A Silent Clock

A Silent Clock

Kevin Ma

iUniverse, Inc.
Bloomington

A Silent Clock

iUniverse books may be ordered through booksellers or by contacting:

iUniverse
1663 Liberty Drive
Bloomington, IN 47403
www.iuniverse.com
1-800-Authors (1-800-288-4677)

ISBN: 978-1-4759-1766-6 (sc)
ISBN: 978-1-4759-1767-3 (ebk)

Printed in the United States of America

iUniverse rev. date: 06/08/2012

CHAPTER 1

I took my initial steps onto the freshly-cut lawn. Both my overconfidence and eagerness outshined my nervousness. As I looked down the rows of cars, I spotted a man in a gray suit and a dark brown cane. He was busy in conversation and seemed to stand out, not just in height. He smiled warmly towards the crowds of zealous parents and students walking over to shake his hand. However, something about the man's demeanor—the overly charming smile that accompanied his concave cheeks—gave me an odd feeling in my gut.

Suddenly, I noticed the aggressive glare from the sun reflecting off the spotless, sparkling cars and shooting directly into my eyes. Nudging me forward, my parents took prideful strides towards the tall man with whom they felt so familiar, my mother and father being alumni and all. The crowd quickly moved towards a lawn on the campus, and I was on edge. I was the only one from my grade school to Kingsley and I didn't know anyone.

Still innocent from the intimidating moments I would come to experience at the Kingsley School, I sat with a straight posture and a bored, impatient attitude in the middle of a long table with white fabric as my parents interacted among others. The large, white tarp that formed a tent, hovering and shading the new families, did nothing to kill the undying heat from the closely packed lines of tables.

I pretended to be engaged in the conversations my parents partook, knowing that sitting and staring at the water droplets that clung to the wet vase filled with golden-yellow tulips in front of me wouldn't speed up the orientation luncheon. Shortly after, the tall man in the gray suit walked up behind a dark, wooden podium. He and the podium rested over the crowd atop an elevated white and blue platform. The man seemed even higher than before compared to us, his seated audience. Only after introducing himself to everyone did I realize he was George Fitzgerald, the headmaster with a well-aged, frail stature but a young face underneath his many wrinkles.

"Ladies and gentlemen, new students and parents, welcome. Today is the day your child embarks on a path towards establishing a very successful future, filled with camaraderie. Whether your son or daughter's journey here is good or great, I can guarantee that the outcome of every student will be brilliant, and I am here to make sure of it. Now, I will admit, this journey will be rigorous, tough, and challenging, but only if each student chooses to follow it. In other words, what happens from here on out, parents, depends solely on your child's determination and choices. To you new students, I address you now. We, at Kingsley, are merely your guides, those who provide the opportunities. However, you, as the incoming new students, have been chosen above others for your responsibility, independence, intelligence, and potential. Now, as my parting words of wisdom, you must prepare for the unexpected, for even the expected may come charging at you if you're not ready. I promise, though, that your time here will all be worth it. Thank you."

I felt a feeling of pride, for my school and in myself. All the while, I couldn't help thinking part of it was bullshit, and that the headmaster had eaten a giant whopping serving of pretentiousness and vomited out at us. Whether this subconscious defiance was towards the headmaster or to me, I was unsure.

As the luncheon died out, so did the clamor of small talk and false laughter. The well-dressed clump gradually dissipated from under the white tent. The students either went into their respective new dormitories or said their last farewells to their parents. I approached my dorm, leaving my parents, who claimed they needed to retire from their day of talking with their old classmates and discussing the school with fresh parents. I knew my father just craved his Blackberry, which he had left behind at the Kingsley Inn on campus.

The hallways of my dorm were filled with busy students and a few parents, all speaking as if they were competing with each other's voices. Upon entering my dorm room, the distinction between the two halves of the room jumped out at me. One section of the space already had been occupied, presumably by my new roommate. The neatly tucked bed sheets and the well-organized desk, humorously enough, shocked me. In my opinion, my half of the room, still bare, held a particular sense of finesse, as far as undecorated walls go.

The eggshell white of the walls and ceiling delivered a dreary atmosphere when the small, dim light bulb turned on. The room was far from spacious, with symmetrical beds and desks. Looming over the room, a large cabinet closet stood in the corner nearly adjacent to the foot of my bed. The narrow entrance to the room was located near my roommate's side with his desk awkwardly encroaching upon any guest's personal space. On top of the dark, cherry workspace was a pocket watch. It was silver on one side, and gold on the other. The subtle ticking exasperated me.

About thirty minutes after I began setting up and organizing my section of the room, I turned around in response to a loud creaking from the opening of the entrance door. A tall kid walked in. Although he wasn't small, he seemed to emanate an indescribably childish glow. He was wearing dirty loafers, a black jacket, stone khakis, and a gray hat that had seen its fair share of use.

"Hi," he spoke in a tone that I can't quite recall. "I'm Micky. Sorry, I already picked one side. I got here last night because my parents drove me up from DC, and we left a little eagerly."

"That's okay, I wanted the right side anyways," I lied.

That night, the dorm collectively met and had a mandatory "bonding" session, courtesy of the house counselor and administrator. People sat, constantly yawning from the pointless sharing of names. The only thing that saved us from entering a state of complete boredom was the cardboard-flavored pizza that was served at the end of the meeting.

As the school week officially began, students either stupidly continued slacking off or ignorantly got their heads right into the paper, not knowing that continuing a diligent study pattern would be nearly unachievable as a human. During study hours, starting at seven thirty each weekday and Sunday nights, the dorms were silent. Although the dorm proctors attempted to enforce this consistent serenity, they honestly didn't care enough to get up from their chairs.

The following nights revealed the eccentricity of my new roommate. He would often disappear for hours and would always come back a few minutes past curfew, rub his pocket watch a few times without ever checking the time in it, and then find some way to procrastinate the rest of his homework, usually by distracting me with wisecracks.

Above anything, he was an apple aficionado, always with the crisp red fruit in hand. Whenever I tried to investigate his whereabouts, he would always reply, "I've just been doing to the same thing you've been."

After a couple of classes, I realized that teachers were as boring as they were corrupt, with the unfair distribution of grades among classes. It was hard to judge what the letter grades truly meant any more. A student could've received an "A" in one class, but were they to move to a lower course with a harsher teacher, they might just as well have received a "B". In many classes, it all came down to how much the instructors liked you. Good grades required a knack for political strategy and not passion or effort.

Time passed by slower each week. It was as if the closer I got to the end of the term, the more stressed I became about making it through. The increasing work seemed to contribute to this irony.

I learned that days only truly seem short in retrospect. Whenever the seniors reflected on their Kingsley careers and spoke about how fast it went by, I understood that it was all just an illusion. In reality, a new weekday only added to the lethargy and despondence that buillt up inside students.

After the painful duration of classes, came sports, which seemed to be designed to suck every last bit of physical energy to challenge a student's endurance for homework. The rainy days and disciplined coaches often added to its struggle.

Of all the different sports available to students, I chose soccer, a sport that I had little experience in, to play in the fall. When it rained, the fields, which had to be shared among numerous teams, turned into quicksand-like muddy messes. When the mud finally dried up, the grass and dirt would turn crusty and uneven, making rolling on ankles far too easy. The practices were long and either boring or exhausting but never in between. Very rarely, though, some mild snowfall would make practice a liability for the school, resulting in cancelled practices and free afternoons that every student treated like valuable possessions.

My only appreciation for soccer practice was when I wasn't playing it. The lengthy duration of games drew out a frustration in me, yet for some inexplicable reason, I still participated in the sport each fall term for the remainder of my career at Kingsley. Looking back, perhaps I chose soccer for its comfort in an attempt to find familiarity.

After practice, dinner at five o'clock became part of my usual routine. In fact, dinner was my favorite part of the day. The Wilkens Commons, where meals were taken, was the most appreciable building, except for its distance from the dorms. The dining hall was spectacularly grandiose in contrast to the dull, uniform red brick buildings around campus. An American and a school flag hung outside, and magnificent blue velvet curtains next to the curved staircases draped from the tall ceilings that relayed even a slight whisper into a loud echo. Marble walls and floors added to the finesse of the culinary ambience that radiated inside. The building always possessed some different exotic grilled meat smell. Further in, long rows of finely crafted and polished wooden tables, which carried a classic aged look with student-carved etches collected from over the years, constantly held platefuls of food in front of students that chattered breathlessly with eagerness to talk. Wilkens earned the respectful title as the only place on campus that could never evoke a bad thought. The food wasn't too detestable, either.

A particular day at Commons seems to emanate the strongest of all my memories, and that was the day when a red circle about the size of a bicycle wheel hung from the ceiling, looking down on all the passersby. I stared at it for what felt like hours, but were likely only seconds, until Micky slapped me back from my trance, "Hey, buddy, you with me?"

I looked at him angrily, "What the hell was that? Did you just slap me?"

"Of course, but I could always punch you in the face, would you like that? I'm sure a slap is sufficient, though," he teased aggressively. "What the hell were you doing anyways? You looked like you were in a trance or something."

Not surprised that he didn't notice something literally right above him, I pointed at the giant circle that hung next to low-hanging chandelier from the tall marble ceiling. He gazed up and cringed in shock, and pure stupidity, "Holy shit! Where did that thing come from?"

I scoffed at Micky's blatant unawareness to his surroundings until a man's voice came from behind us, "Almost hypnotic, isn't it?"

Headmaster Fitzgerald stood with his hands in his pockets and a suit slightly grayer than what I remember during orientation. He looked a lot taller and lankier close up than from a distance. He stood comfortably with his cane and rectangular glasses, giving himself a debonair sophistication that almost disgusted me.

"What is it?" Micky asked without changing his focus, mesmerized by the simple shape.

"Why this belongs to the Red Clock Order, gentlemen," Fitzgerald said, pointing his cane above him.

Micky's eyes lit up conspicuously as he heard the "Red Clock Order". I decided to ignore it temporarily, understanding that, while I definitely disliked this headmaster, it's best not to make a bad first impression. It's all politics, right?

The headmaster chuckled, "Of all things, however, this society is perhaps the only part of school that I have no knowledge of. All I know is that they hang up this large clock, painted over with red, twice a year. The large majority of its rich history is kept secret. Quite a shame."

"Wait," I interrupted, "secret societies don't exist anymore."

For a couple seconds, he held the same mesmerized look towards the clock as Micky did, before looking back down at me. "Ah, Thomas. I recall speaking with your parents during orientation. They were quite the individuals. Anyhow, as far as anyone is concerned, they don't exist. There's nothing we can do about it, though, if we don't know who's behind it. As long as people don't get hurt, and the school doesn't lose a drastic amount of money, then it's not an issue.

"I was in the same class as your father, Thomas. Your mother is also a good acquaintance of mine. She is quite the lovely woman. Your parents wanted me to watch out for you, make sure that you didn't get into trouble," he continued.

I seethed under my false smile and chuckle, "Thank you sir, but I don't plan on getting into too much of that here."

The headmaster gave me a momentary contemplative stare before returning the fake smile and chuckle, "Well I don't believe that you would. Just make sure you watch out. Boarding school sometimes tends to be too much for certain students. Well, I'll see you boys later. Have a good evening."

Micky, barely having left his trance between himself and the clock, returned to reality after Mr. Fitzgerald left, "Well that's weird."

"Yeah, I don't really like that guy," I replied.

"Who?" Micky asked confused, "I was talking about the clock."

The rest of the dinner was filled with random conversation, avoiding the subject of the large red clock that Micky seemed so fond of and humbled by. As the plates of burnt chicken, mashed potatoes, and chewy carrots emptied, we took the long journey back to the dorm. Eventually, curiosity got the best of me, "What was that clock thing all about?" I asked abruptly.

"What? The Red Clock?" Micky asked without a stutter in his step.

"Yeah, the giant one hanging from the Commons ceiling," I replied, "What's the Red Clock?"

Excitement and admiration filled his voice, "You mean the Red Clock Order? It's the school's oldest secret society. I heard about it when I was visiting this school. My father told me about it when I was young. They pick you, you don't pick them, and they have an affinity for the academically gifted and athletically astounding type. It sounds kind of lame."

"So what do they do, the Red Clock folks, I mean?" I asked, skeptic about the magnificence of the society I just heard about twenty minutes ago.

Micky slowed down his pace, "I don't know . . . they meet. I know that they have a lot of connections, and that the old alumni members donate a ton of money to the school. If anything, it's just an elitist group founded by the school to profit off the pride of wealthy alumni. But wouldn't it be awesome to be a part of it?" He seemed interested, but I had little concern and scoffed his question away.

Friday morning, dozens of small alarm clocks with their faces painted red were placed near the steps towards Commons. During the day, freshmen and new students chattered on and wondered about the fiasco that took place in the morning. A number of arrogant upperclassmen responded as if they were themselves members, explaining how the clocks meant that new members had been officially inducted as the ruling members of the Red Clock Order. The more I heard about this "Order", the more it sounded like a cult and the more I questioned its purpose. The more that this secret society did, the more they seemed like a group of high school students desperate for more attention by flaunting their reputation and money.

Micky's curiosity for this society, however, grew more and more with time. It was, evidently, something that had peaked his awareness for a while. When passing by, he would stare at Galloway House, the meeting house that sheltered all the pretentious bastards while they discussed their easy futures. The building's exterior was nothing impressive, but it leeched its resonating glory through the rich legacies that entered it.

I couldn't understand its appeal then, believing that it was only an exclusive clubhouse. Part of my disgust may have actually been jealousy from the fact that I wasn't a part of it. Being born under the roof of a prosperous family, my father was well connected with wealthy associates. Therefore, I was always a part of expensive dinner parties held by high executive golfing partners of my father's ever since I grew old enough to know not to shout in front of guests. I had always been part of the inner circle.

Back when he had some time to care, my father brought me along to his work events in hopes that I would get a head start on building good connections for my own future. Since then, after meeting individuals with multi-million-dollar salaries, I always had a secret, hidden pride and belief of superiority. The Red Clock Order appeared too far-fetched of a dream, and so it wasn't worth the effort.

When the night arrived, Micky's stupidity reached an all time high. We sat around in a spacious single room where two boys in our class, Big Ed and Jerry, lived. When I first met the two, I thought they were brothers. Both were just over six feet with muscular builds and enormous feet. The differences were visible in their hair and attitudes, however.

Big Ed had brown hair and always attempted to convey a rough demeanor whereas Jerry was a ginger and was almost sadistically nice. Together they were a calamitous pair of roommates. One time, they even got into an aggressive fight with each other over a Twinkie bar they found in the dorm common room.

Micky had first befriended Jerry for his mischievous behavior, which my roommate mistook as a playful personality. "He's a laid back kid," Micky commented about Jerry, after I defined the guy as "bad news".

On that particular weekend night, Micky picked up a few baseballs lying on the floor and began to start juggling them around, "Hey, what do you guys think about trying to sneak into the Clockroom?"

"The what?" I questioned.

"You know, that place in Galloway House where the members all meet."

At this point, I realized that understanding the complex workings of Micky's stupidity was pointless, and that I just had to sit back and accept it with a chuckle and a mild grin.

I tried to avoid his attention to prevent the risk of him volunteering me to go inside.

"You're crazy," Big Ed said as he futilely tried to sharpen a pencil without breaking it, "That sounds like a lot of bad news that would come our way if we get caught."

"I'm not crazy," Micky denied, "Don't you want to know what the hell's inside that place? I mean, they're clearly begging for more attention with all the stuff they do. It must be pretty cool inside their place."

"Yeah. I say we do it," Jerry proposed with a contemplating tone while staring down at the carpeted floor full of spilled crumbs and dirty laundry. He had always been a fanatic for disobedience, and his insolence was blatant, even in front of parents or faculty. He sneered, "I don't think we'd get caught. But I mean think about it, if we snuck in and did something like stole the Red Clock, we'd be legends, bigger than Big Ed's Sasquatch hands."

It seemed stupid that this discussion was even still continuing, but I had nowhere else to go. Meanwhile, Micky's and Jerry's spontaneous dream grew more powerful with each comment.

Big Ed glared at him before continuing his failed pencil sharpening, "We'd be in a lot of trouble, if not with the teachers then with the people in the—"

"So it's decided, we're going in," Micky jumped in. He left the room momentarily and the door closed behind him. Confused, we all waited in awkward silence. Thirty seconds later, Micky barged back in holding a few straws from the broom in the common room, and the door handle smacked a minor indent into the wall, "We'll draw straws to see who goes."

"Wait, wait, wait," I interjected, "you're not actually considering doing this, are you?"

"Yeah, I don't think we should send a good kid like Tom into the wild," Jerry added. I glared at him.

Micky dismissed Jerry with a twitch of his hand, "You mean are *we* doing this, and yes, we are. Don't be a pansy, Tommy boy. If you don't draw this straw, then I'll draw it for you."

"No, I didn't agree to this," I blurted.

Unfortunately, it was too late, and Micky drew out the second shortest straw, and drew out, for me, the shortest.

"You've got to be kidding me," I muttered.

"Well, how about that?" Jerry admired, giving me a quick pat on the back, "good luck, bud."

From the room in Jerry's window, Galloway House was visible. The moment the light in the building was on, the three who I considered my friends came bursting into my room. Micky convinced me to leave the house, and dragged me towards Galloway while I struggled and begged to return to the dorm.

"Go on, you have to do it. You knew what you were getting yourself into when we drew the straws!" Micky said as he pushed me toward the small, yet intimidating building. I always believed that his insisting attitude would get the best of him one day. "Don't worry, we'll watch your back."

I made my way to the house, nearly slipping a few times on the watery snow of late fall. By habit, I placed my hand on the door about to knock, but was halted by Micky's loud whispering, which could easily match anyone's typical yelling voice.

"What are you doing? You're not a goddamn guest. Just go inside and do it quietly, for Christ's sake," Micky blurted.

What had I gotten into? I thought. It'd have been a better choice to just wait outside in the hallway and wait for Micky's wild imaginations to consume himself. But, being the innocent and naïve child I was sophomore year, it seemed like just some harmless mischief.

With a mocking smile back at Micky, I opened the door. Surprised that it was unlocked, I stepped inside and closed the door softly behind me. The room appeared twice as large on the inside as it did on the outside. One large chandelier hung, barely, over the room and brightly lit the area. Unfortunately, I had little time to admire the intricacies of interior design until loud footsteps made their way closer to the door on the other side of the room. With nothing to hide behind but a few tables and a coat hanger, I jumped to a small space in the far left corner. A row of people then exited the door, all finely dressed in pristine dark blazers.

A large, well-dressed person, however, approached my no-longer-safe niche under the stairs. He hovered just under seven feet and had a large build. This figure who was glowering at me was Jacob MacCarry, captain of the school's heavyweight rowing team and Harvard recruit. His face and size were recognizable by any student on campus. My forehead only reached his shoulders, so all I could see was a noticeable well-stitched patch of a red circle with golden laurels on his dark jacket's right chest.

"You're not allowed in here," MacCarry muttered with a heavy, rumbling voice. He picked me up, carried me to the front door and threw me back outside.

The sound of my ass hitting the gravel drew the attention of the people that had just exited Galloway House. They turned around and one of them confidently, or rather arrogantly, walked towards me with a malicious grin, "What do we have here?" He crouched down as others gathered around me.

"I found him trying to head up to the Clockroom," MacCarry informed the others.

"Clockroom?" the other guy replied. He was skinny and pale, like a stretched out piece of dough. Red hair covered his triangular face. He appeared no older than me, and he had a face that I'd just love to punch. "I say we ought to teach him a lesson," he suggested, likely more to himself than to everyone else. He balled his hands up into a tight fist. "That's a nice tie, kiddo," he remarked, "It'd look better with some red on it."

Before I could open my mouth to babble gibberish in an attempt to dissuade his oncoming fist, his hand blurred. Next thing I knew, I was lying on the ground with a nose that started bleeding profusely. Seconds later, his fist rose above me again. This time, luckily for me, someone interceded what I imagine would've been more excruciating than the first punch. "Take it easy, bud." The man looked aged but not frail. No hair was present on the top of his head and a classic tweed jacket hid his probably sweaty pits. I didn't recognize him at the time.

As my head throbbed and the crowd walked away, I stood up and spit the metallic taste of blood from my mouth. Micky and the rest of the group in hiding rushed out from the bushes afterwards. "Thanks for the help," I mumbled sarcastically with what I guessed was a broken tooth.

"Those guys were big as hell, Tommy boy," he excused, "We would've gotten our asses kicked."

"Yeah, right," I said, supporting my still aching head.

For the long walk back to my dorm, I tuned out what I imagined was Micky's nonsensical ranting and cleaned the blood profusely pouring from my face.

"Did you get it?" Micky asked with fervor in his tone.

"What?" I replied in an as blatantly upset voice as I could create.

"The Clock."

"What do you think?" I replied angrily, "Does it look like I have the fucking Clock?"

"Why not?" Micky asked, with not an inch of lost excitement in him.

I glared at him intently; until I finally accepted his idiocy, "Fuck you, that's why."

So began my career at Kingsley. Only the first term, and already I had a bloody nose from a punch. Never had I been punched before, or even met someone so outright impertinent as the ginger kid that hit me.

As a new sophomore, it was difficult not to stand out from the returnees. It soon became a club, a society even, consisting of new sophomores that dwelled in reclusion and away from the veterans sophomores, who had been here as freshman. The one thing that all students experienced, old and new alike, was the foggy, wet, autumn New Hampshire days that weakened the spirits of any who attended Kingsley. Constant heavy, overcast and mild rain, from the early morning to the school's strict nine o' clock campus wide curfew. The rain gave the students a dreary feeling that drove some to the border of seasonal depression. Fighting through the endless terror of new work and stern teachers grew increasingly difficult with each passing day as well.

CHAPTER 2

After sports one Tuesday afternoon, I headed up to Commons when Micky ran up from the varsity fields. It would not have been unusual, or even rude to deem Micky bizarre or stupid upon meeting him. What didn't show, however, was his exceptional athletic ability buried underneath the lazy, skinny kid, with annoying confidence, who practically had a hole under his jaw considering the amount of food that spilled out when he ate. He paid interest to only the most peculiar of things and had a weak common sense that could never keep up with his true academic potential or intelligence.

His inexplicable high grades fueled a competitive drive inside me, one that was not easy to be contained. But he and I were friends, regardless of my mild rivalry, one that I don't think Micky felt as strongly about.

"You going to dinner after lockers?" Micky asked as he sprinted awkwardly with a large grin and his oversized gym bag flapping behind. His cheek muscles didn't seem to have the capability of relaxing except in his sleep, and maybe not even then. Many times, his incessant upbeat attitude irritated me to the core, but on occasion it was hilarious. He could trip over backwards and still be talking about how he heard some man in Indonesia supposedly had a tongue that was six feet long.

"Yeah," I replied, tired with dried sweat sticking to my skin, "but I need to go to the scheduling office to change my history class afterwards."

"What's wrong with the one that you're in now?" Micky asked staring blankly at the grass in front of him. I could tell that at this point, his mind had already begun to drift off.

"It's too easy, all the teacher does is throw dates at you," I told him.

"I don't see the problem," he paused. "Dates are tasty." I couldn't tell if his remark was serious or not.

"Not that kind. It's just the one that messes with your mind. I already memorized those historical dates years ago. It's not at all useful," I replied with a complaining tone.

Micky abruptly stopped in his tracks and looked over, "Well you're just so special, aren't you?" he said with a joking sarcasm, and then, expecting me to keep up, he immediately broke into a fast-paced trot.

I envied Micky's endless capacity for energy. In contrast, I always ended up pent up inside my small white, hospital-like dorm room that was only missing bars on the windows in order to be classified as an insane asylum. The dark, dusty desk, from eight at night to two in the morning, was my hub of solitary confinement as I spent endless hours of the night writing, erasing, and rewriting the infinitely increasing pile of homework.

From dinner, I rushed straight to the offices before they closed. A woman sat down to discuss my schedule for nearly half an hour, talking about how it was a very complicated procedure and would require some courses I was already in to change periods. I was fine with it and didn't understand what the big deal was.

By nine o'clock, I returned home to my creaking chair and intimidating desk, with my work laid out in front of me. A pink course change slip, signed by the scheduling desk, sat next to my folders. The writing that looked faded from the tip of a ballpoint pen with a low supply of ink read "Course

Change—Thomas Walther—Request: Remove History 2, Add History 3—Signed: Scheduling Counselor Wendy Bishop, Signed: Administrator Hastings." I didn't know what exactly an administrator was, or what power they possessed, but I was just glad to have been able to leave the history class that I currently had. To be honest, I had no idea what the higher class taught, or if I could keep up with the course. But my teacher's crude, condescending remarks towards students and his smiles reserved only for girls in low-cut dresses and short skirts exacerbated me to the core and hampered the efficiency of my performance. So I had no real choice but to switch out.

The rest of the night was filled with a clutter of crumpled papers inside open textbooks. With all the work that I had, only two weeks into school, I could find little time to organize the disarray of food, plastic wrappers, and torn paper inside my confined space the school considered a room. The word "In" neatly adorned the top left corner of a sheet of paper titled "Gatsby's Contrasting Character Evolution with the Buchanan Family". The title itself was by no means my choice, and the paper was just waiting to be torn up, so I didn't even see the point in writing it.

That night, when Micky just wouldn't stop opening and closing his pocket watch, I just had to ask, "Cut it out. What's that goddamn watch for, anyways? It's a piece of crap, throw it out."

"This thing? My good ol' grandpappy got me this. Trust me, I've thought about throwing it out, I mean, I have no use for it, but I just can't bear to do it," Micky replied with sentiment, but little else, in his voice.

Embarrassed by my rude comment, I decided to bury myself under my textbooks for the rest of the night without speaking another word. I sat for a good thirty minutes before finally getting thoughts out.

Symbolism always frustrated me. If a man wanted to convey a message, there was no need to hide it behind hundreds of pages. If anything, using symbolism weakened the message and created too many opportunities for open interpretation in which all paths inevitably result in conflict. My momentary rage towards symbolism drew from my frustration towards the English paper. The course was too subjective and I wasn't creative enough.

Next morning, I almost arrived at second period late. Having slept through my alarm and first period after working for hours on a single assignment due in one night, I walked into my new history class gasping for breath from the long run to the building from my dorm. Inside, the empty classroom was cold with thin carpeting and dark wooden walls. The glossy desks made a perfect semi-circle around a large teacher's desk. Behind that desk sat a middle-aged man wearing an olive tweed jacket and elbow patches. After looking at his partially bald, shiny dome, I realized that this man was the exact same person who had left Galloway house the night I was punched.

The man looked up from a stack of papers and removed his circular reading glasses, "Hi, I'm Dr. Carter. Have a seat." He pushed his chair back and stood up, walking over to shake my hand, "You must be Mr. Walther."

I nodded as he continued on with a dim smile and emotionless stare, "The administrator told me you were coming. Well, it's a pleasure to meet you."

He came over to me and placed a stapled, two-page class syllabus on my desk. There was no way that he didn't recognize me, so I began to grow almost frustrated that he chose not to mention that incident only two nights ago when one of the students almost kicked my ass all the way to the hospital.

As the next couple minutes passed, he waited for the remainder of the students to arrive. I felt angry, worried, and hungry all at the same time, but hunger seemed to dominate the majority of my mind after sleeping through breakfast. The only thing that momentarily sustained me from entering starvation was the taste of spearmint in the back of my throat from when I accidentally swallowed some chewing gum in an attempt to get rid of morning breath while running to class.

By the end of the history class, I had little energy left. My eyelids, throughout the hour-long class, faced an endless battle with my semi-conscious brain in a tiring skirmish to control the border of sleep and awareness. History 3 had little difference between it and its lower courses, except this class threw twice as many dates from the short duration of human history.

Just as I fully left my daze behind in the classroom, Dr. Carter's big, hairy hand landed on my right shoulder, "Mr. Walther, enjoy the class?"

In courses where grades are not fully determined by specific percentages, a leeway of one or more letter grades is possible. By the end of each of the school year's three terms, the final grade in these courses are determined subjectively, so a form of kiss-ass politics has grown more and more necessary. It was, at the very least, nice to have a teacher care, even though Carter probably had some dwelling dislike for me for sneaking into Galloway House.

I prepared myself to bullshit. All I remembered before I stopped paying attention was the mention of the House of Wisdom—a lesson I had already learned freshman year at my previous school—underlined and written in large across the whiteboard. I took a deep, but quiet sigh and turned around with a heavy mask of civility, "Yes, sir, Dr.

Carter. I enjoyed your lecture on the destruction of the Bayt Al-Hikmah by the Mongols in the thirteenth century. It's too bad all those books were lost."

"Indeed," the aging teacher took a slight pause with a conspicuous stare. I suspected he was judging me for a few seconds before he spoke again, "Yes, well, all information ends up somewhere. For the Arabs, it was the scholars and people that spread the words written on the paper. For Kingsley, it's some students at this school that have the potential to upkeep the traditions and strengths of the school's society, perhaps one unbeknownst entirely to most others."

His naturally serious face created a disarmingly hospitable smile, "Well, I won't hold you any longer. Have a happy Monday."

Slightly dazed and confused about the conversation that I just participated in, I walked slowly to third period math. The next few hours of the day seemed to pass by in an instant, a long dragged-out instant.

Teachers just didn't realize that just droning on to students for endless amounts of time could not allow us to retain information. Come summertime, about half of what I learned would have disappeared.

Unfortunately, as soon as the long term began, it seemed to end. When every day seemed to have the same processes of eating, studying, and sleeping, it became hard to remember which day was which until the end came near. Before final exams week would be the short, weeklong intermission of Thanksgiving.

It was deceiving, however. Students would often prepare early and cram from their textbooks back home, while the warm scent of roast turkey would provide the illusion that it was truly "break". Thanksgiving turkey, gravy, and stuffing provided a momentary hiatus from classes, but not work, before returning once more to the school of countless homework in order to complete final exams.

My own family would take turns hosting at the houses of different family members for Thanksgiving each year. To my disappointment, it was my aunt's turn to host my first Thanksgiving back from Kingsley. Instead of sleeping and studying at home while caterers prepared the evening meal, my mother drove us up to northern Massachusetts while I got carsick from reading in the car. My father did not attend, as it was typical of him to only ever attend Thanksgiving when it was held at home. He never liked to stray too far from his office.

During Thanksgiving dinner, when I had gotten slightly buzzed from a few bottles of beer, I faced a barrage of questions by my family about school. "How's school? Are you having fun? Do you have a lot of work?" aunts and uncles would ask. "It's great. Yes, I'm having tons of fun. There's some work, but not too much," I would fib in response.

The truth is that, were there actually time to perform any meaningful enjoyable task at school, it would've likely been replaced with studying, anyways. Of course, I didn't mind telling these stories and white lies, since they made the eyes of my aunts and uncles glisten from joyful reminiscing of boarding school in their youth.

My mother urged me to get a head start in studying over break in hopes of scoring better than other students. Even though I knew that other students had likely already began their finals preparations and that I now found extreme difficulty in focusing on work anywhere outside of the my dorm room, I acquiesced to my mother's recommendation.

Upon returning to Kingsley and beginning final exams, I questioned my own ability to finish even one question on the exam. No matter how much I skimmed the textbooks or reviewed the past tests, anxiety corrupted any small strings of confidence that I had in my knowledge. No one spoke a word on campus for the four days of tests, ninety minutes each. Each sudent invested precious time in chemistry, history . . . until, at long last, the sweet three-week respite from hard work arrived to release the pressure building up.

The day that I returned home after the eaxms, the fragrance of perfume and dog food that had once smelled so familiar to me now smelled strange and foreign. Only my parents and the greeting from my oversized Australian shepherd, Cooper, provided any hint of familiarity. The ceaseless chatter of my mother and the stench of Cooper's breath brought me somewhat out of the shell that I'd been hiding in over the past eight weeks.

Without legitimate studying to do every night, the holiday vacation passed by relatively slowly in comparison to school. Each day took forever to pass by, and the inactivity from not having to walk long distances between classes every day made me feel slothful.

By the middle of vacation, nights spilled into days, and vice versa, and I enjoyed sleeping close to twelve hours a day. With fresh homemade food on the table every night and a car to travel in, there was little I could do to complain. Yet no matter how dull and monotonous my first term had seemed, I couldn't help but feel fervent about the idea of returning. Interestingly enough, my mindset toward Kingsley changed the moment I stepped foot on campus again.

The roads, paved with ice, caused highway congestion and delayed my arrival by car until dusk. A dry, blistering breeze chilled me to the core when I stepped out of the car only wearing a light windbreaker as an ineffective form of insulation.

Micky's side of the bedroom was as messy as the day he had left for vacation, with half of his blanket lying on the ground. His desk was cluttered with old quizzes, each with large A's on the top corner. Only his pocket watch rested neatly on the center of his nightstand. Micky walked in with an apple in his hand a couple minutes after I had started unpacking and clapped his hands in excitement, "Hey, Tommy boy's back!" He started walking out in the halls yelling that for a few minutes until a proctor finally shouted back at him to shut up or receive an earlier curfew on the first week of winter classes. Dorm camaraderie had never felt so good.

"You're crazy," I scoffed at him after he came back in from his deranged shouting spree. "How was break?" I asked trying to be a normal person in order to counterbalance the insanity that my roommate brought in.

Completely ignoring the question, Micky grabbed my football and chucked it towards me. The football hit my stomach and nearly knocked the wind out of my lungs. "Bud, you don't call or write? What's that all about?"

"Jesus, I didn't realize I was in a long-term relationship," I joked while trying to throw the football back at him, but I missed and nearly left a deep dent in the drywall above his desk.

At that moment, Jerry barged in with Big Ed following behind him, "Well, well, if it isn't 'Tommy boy' himself. What dissidence against the Red Clock Order are we planning on taking up now?"

Micky jumped up from his desk, "Don't put the blame on him, it was my idea." He clearly felt offended for someone else receiving credit for his preposterous proposal last fall to try and invade the Clockroom. "As the mastermind, I say we give it another go, put our seasoned veteran back in," he said as he nodded towards me.

To avoid any risk of ending up punched in the face again, I got up and left to go to the bathroom. When I went back in a minute later, Micky, who was the only person left in the room, looked over with an almost malicious smile, "Good news, we've agreed to put you back in the frontlines."

"No," I refuted in disbelief.

"Yes," Micky replied, with his consistently energetic tone.

"Listen, I don't know if all those apples that you've been eating have some alien that's now inside you controlling your brain, or if you're just that stupid to begin with, but I'm not going back in there!" I said in a trembling voice, "I can't believe Jerry and Ed agreed to this, too, those bastards."

Storming into Jerry and Ed's room, I could've sworn steam was coming out of my ears. "You guys are fucking retards."

Jerry stood up and walked towards the closet nonchalantly hanging up his light brown wool blazer, "Slow down there. What are you talking about?"

"After getting beaten up the first time, I'd have thought that you guys wouldn't be stupid enough to have Micky convince you to make me do it again," I spat, not caring who else heard through the thin, hollow walls between rooms.

Jerry stared at me with puzzlement while Big Ed scoffed and kept on working on his homework, "I have no idea what you're talking about. We left the room pretty much right after you did."

Suddenly aware of my uncontrolled outburst, I felt extremely embarrassed. I was lost and completely bewildered by what just occurred, until Micky approached me with a large smile, which nearly consumed half his face.

Then, I realized the obnoxious prank that my exasperating roommate had played on me the first night back to school.

It took all the self-restraint I possessed to not punch him. So sparked the beginning of my hatred towards my roommate.

"You're crazy, Micky," I said, shaking my head in disappointment. He just laughed in delirium.

Part of me commended him for being able to disguise his true personality well enough for the interviewer to provide a good recommendation to Kingsley. The other part, the sensible portion, could not comprehend how a student as eccentric and dense as Micky could perform adequately in class.

I went to bed at around eleven that night, well before anyone else, in an attempt to feel well-rested the next day. The morning arrived with the pleasant view of a fresh new blanket of snow, gently decorating the surface of the campus lawn. However, my room was not nearly as delightful. The house counselor had posted a note in the hallway, explaining that the school would not turn on its heating services until two days later.

Until then, an unheated dorm room provided little warmth and satisfaction on a cold winter morning. The large window between our two beds spilled in frigid air like a broken dam. I looked over at Micky, who was sleeping soundly. With a nice kick to his side, he woke up promptly, muttering indiscernible gibberish. This added humor to the start of my day.

Every morning, my legs woke up stiff and my awareness hazy. Provided one had a thick, snow proof jacket and heavy boots, the layers of snow proved to be a nice change from the dull atmosphere of fall overcasts and muddy asphalt. But like anything enjoyable, the blinding reflective sheet of untouched snow, which made sunglasses a necessity in the wintertime, would quickly turn into slush until the next snowfall.

After a typical mid-winter day, when I had slipped twice on the steps near the history building, which the custodians had failed to salt properly, I made my way through a long trudge away from main campus towards James Athletic Center, the indoor fields and hockey rink.

I could never bear the sound of sharp metal skates scraping the cold ice floor, nor could I accomplish the challenging feat of multitasking adept skating with brutal body checks. So I discovered that squash, the polar opposite of hockey, would be a suitable, albeit mediocre, alternative as a second term sport.

The sport was gratefully made co-ed, with no limitation for participants. Apparently the Head of the Atheletic Department, John Wyatt, a man with a rugged beard and faded, eccentric white hair, was worried that there would not be enough participants in one gender to create an entire recreational squash group. He was wrong.

The first day inside the clean, albeit uncomfortably heated, squash courts, there was little opportunity for playing time due to the amount of people that had signed up. Of course, I didn't complain, nor did a large majority of the group that took advantage of the disorganization and took much needed naps on the benches.

The court's fresh-paint smell and lucid glass doors made me believe that this portion of the gym was a new addition. While I appreciated it then, I would later come to learn that Kingsley was always undergoing some sort of renovation to liven the dull uniformity on campus. Usually, the construction was just an attempt to reverse the deterioration of a building that was critical in the history of the school. This time, however, rust had grown into the pipes in the squash courts, requiring destruction of walls. The construction required the school to receive permission from the trustees to dip into the massive endowment in order to recreate a useless portion of an otherwise modern building.

A couple days later, the squash instructor, who was a French teacher with a reputation for not giving two shits about teaching by day, finally placed me in against someone, a girl. Theoretically, I should've complained, except my zero years, zero months, and zero days experience in the "sport" prevented me from doing so with proper justification. The girl had a plain yet competitive face and blond hair tightly wound into a ponytail. Combined with the mandatory plastic goggles, white polo shirt, and uncomfortably short unisex shorts for practice, her guise conveyed an intimidating, almost professional appearance.

"Elise Poitier! Thomas Walth-er! Second court, hurry up," the husky squash instructor huffed between wheezes. I winced after witnessing his spittle residue hit the backside of a student after he mispronounced my surname but not "Poitier's".

"I'll try to go easy," I teased jokingly to the girl as I stepped into the court.

She gave a stern look before realizing that I was joking and provided a barely visible smile in response, "We'll see."

I lost zero to eleven. I had planned out my excuse to tell everyone that I didn't bother to try while actually convincing myself that that was honestly the reason. The occasion, however, never arose that required me to say so, considering how little anyone cared and how few people actually were watching.

After the game, my superior opponent approached me with a triumphant modesty, "Thanks for going easy on me," she said in a playful arrogance.

Without a witty response, I left smiling, but felt abashed and regretful at my incompetence with repartee, something beneficial that would not be entirely inappropriate to teach in the school curriculum. Although the first time that I encountered her was only when we were both drenched in sweat, not from intensity but from an excessively generous gymnasium central heating system, there was something about her. As per usual, though, my work buried any thoughts about her deeply away.

CHAPTER 3

Every moment at Kingsley so far had felt disconnected. Each day, I hoped to be a part of something exciting, unordinary, or bizarre, so that I wouldn't have to rub my eyes and temples from staring down at my desk with a deep frustration. My god, if this what the rest of life was really like, I'd never have agreed to participate in it.

Although I detested all these assignments, my own whining about the amount of essays and homework irked me even more, but it had seemed that complaining about work was a fundamental part of experiencing and developing in boarding school.

I was sitting in history one day when I fell asleep, once again. "Mr. Walther," my history teacher bellowed, "perhaps you should invest in some more hours of sleep or maybe coffee." A couple snickers went around the classroom after this comment.

Dr. Carter and I had never discussed the night I snuck into Galloway House, and I couldn't tell if his distaste towards me and mine towards him was due to this unspoken event or if it was due to my disinterest in his course. Either the morning or the lackluster class was causing me to fall asleep during history every day. It was probably the class's fault, I firmly believed.

"I'm sorry, Dr. Carter, I suppose nine in the morning is too inconceivable for my adolescent brain." A few more chortles by classmates were audible.

"Yes, well if Constantine or Genghis Khan thought the way you did, I don't think man would have gotten very far," Dr. Carter replied with a taunting smirk. Uproarious cackling filled every inch of the room.

With a perfect response in mind, I enunciated above the guffawing, "With all due respect, sir, I'd rather choose naptime over war." The room was silent. Out of my own egotistical self-righteousness, I believed that the other students were actually nodding in their minds.

With a glass full of pride, I intently relished in my unspoken victory until a thick left hand settled onto my right shoulder and my startled reaction shattered my haughtiness. "Mr. Walther," Dr. Carter used his mammoth hand to force me around, "I'm sure you've seen this coming, but we must discuss the matter of your grades in my course."

My heart dropped and I unconsciously gulped some air. This was the last thing I wanted to deal with, and the most important thing to upkeep, in my mind. "My grades? Is there something wrong?" I asked nervously.

"From the look on your face and the tone in your voice, you don't know what this discussion entails exactly. Well, your grades are neither unacceptable nor failing, but are still somewhat low for this class," I couldn't tell whether or not he was finding satisfaction in telling me this. His face showed sincerity, but I'd learned better than to trust a face.

"Take heed that you are in a higher course than many of your peers. You aren't required to move down, but I've filed a notice to the administrator of the possibility. You are free to choose, but if you decide that you want to move halfway into the term, you may fall behind," he concluded and extended his arm out, expecting a handshake. With a responsibility to the student part inside of me, which had been buried somewhere deep inside my head after this conversation, I reluctantly extended my arm out as well.

From what I remember, I was so focused on being infuriated with the teacher that I didn't realize the piece of paper left in my hand until I tried to push open the door leading to the main hallway of the building and the paper dropped from my hand. I unfolded the crisp sheet of white paper and skimmed only the first page. Notwithstanding the fact that I was the unspoken victor of the previous contretemps, I somehow still ended up with an extra assignment in my hand.

I walked into my room and got to work on my new history assignment. A few hours later, frustrated and tired, I announced to Micky, "That guy plays favorites, I know it. Either that or he hates me with a passion. I'm not a bad student; there are plenty of other people who do a lot worse and who don't even try to stay awake in class. Doesn't it sound like this guy hates me?"

Micky walked in with an apple in his hand seconds after I asked him, and I realized that he hadn't actually been in the room. I had been talking to no one.

"Where do you keep getting those apples?" I asked.

"What do you mean?" Micky wondered between chews, with a loud crunch of the apple crushing between his molars with every bite, "I get it from Commons."

"Forget it," I surrendered.

Crumpling another piece of paper and tossing it near or around, but never in, my wastebasket, I took a heavy sigh and rubbed my eyes and temples. Micky turned around in his chair slowly, "You know, if you throw another piece of crumpled paper next to your trash can, your floor will look like one of those rooms in those corny movies. I can see it now," Micky said, making a rectangular frame with his fingers, mimicking an announcer, "Thomas Walther is the big man on campus. He was the big man on campus, the captain of the baseball team, but, it turns out, he was born with the brain the size of a peanut! To keep playing sports, he's only got sixty days to get his grade up. This winter, directed by Oscar-award winning actor and director, Micky Jones, comes the best bad movie you've ever seen. Sounds like a hit, doesn't it, Tommy boy?"

I laughed with a hint of weariness. The night had drained all vitality from my blood and brain, leaving me in an unstable state of hysteria. "I'm going to be honest with you, Micky, I probably wouldn't find this funny were it not . . ." I paused to check my alarm clock, "one in the morning. Damn it. How do you do it, anyways? I've never seen you throw a bad test onto your desk so far."

The delightful lunatic lost his chipper luster for a moment and shrugged, "I just do the same thing you do. I study."

"Now I know that's not true," I rejected, "you're gone for hours after dinner, and I barely see you do any work afterwards. You must have some secret, some super power."

Micky gave a loud, hearty laughter that nearly shook the building, "If I did have one, then I'd be pissed off since no one told me about it. Why are you suddenly so obsessed with trying to figure this out, anyways?"

"Because!" I responded in a wild desperation, hoping for some magic secret, "It's been maybe only four months of school, a few weeks into winter term, and I already feel as if my head's about to explode!"

"Calm down," Micky replied, with two words that I never thought he would tell someone else, "I don't have a secret. I'm just an efficient worker. You're not that diligent of a student yourself, pal. Every time I see you doing homework, you always go to the bathroom, take a nap, or go off chatting."

"By God!" I joked faintly, "What happened to my roommate, destitute of common sense? He's been replaced with a sensible, maniacal monster! Why are you even still awake?"

Micky smiled and turned back in his chair to pick up his pocket watch, "Same thing you're doing, Tommy boy."

Whether it was by some deep insatiable jealous instinct or the madness of living with a roommate, I always felt a deep competitive urge against Micky. His lackadaisical study habits and mysterious disappearances still provided him with the satisfying grades that I strived to achieve. I, on the other hand, always faced stressful challenges, which I often grumbled about as my papers gently spelled out my increasingly pathetic future in sinful red ink. I understood that Micky wasn't the smartest student, but I felt that beating him academically would be a fulfilling achievement.

As I crawled into bed that night, having brushed my teeth for barely a second, thoughts of incomplete, inadequate work filled my head, which only irritated me more. I only hoped that the administrator, some unknown higher figure, would not see my faults on paper or even relegate me back down to the even more insipid and simplistic teachings of second level history.

If that class didn't provide enough gray hair and bags under my eyes, I always had my French class, where my teacher danced around and made fun of others but never actually taught anything useful; my math class, where my teacher stood in front of a chalkboard and droned for an hour while he wrote meaningless equations on the board; or even art class, where my teacher's bullshit knew no bounds in analyzing pieces of clay. Any of those classes presented me with the stress that I learned to hate.

The acclaimed better education of a preparatory school was, in fact, only deceptively beneficial to a student. Maybe the school taught me to work hard, but the regular sleepless nights and anxiety put a heavy toll on my health. Everything that I did was for college, to get into a good one, so the immense disparity of difficulty between here and at a local private school would hopefully have been outweighed by its memories, although very few were worth remembering thus far. The hard-earned money from my parents paid only for the food and the boarding school experience, not for the acceptance letter to a good college.

Considering the detestable food at Commons and the overpriced delivery charges from local restaurants, the experience, which was yet to be benefited from, was the only thing of value to look forward to. To be honest, I loved diminishing the actual value of studying at Kingsley with my constant ranting. It made me feel that all this stress wasn't my fault, but back then, I actually made myself believe what I said was true.

In the midst of complaining about school in my head, I dozed off and slept through my alarm until two minutes before class started.

Given the unpredictability of grades, fate of all things became a wild religion of mine, which I believed often factored into foreshadowing the positive or negative outcomes of classes for the day. As I struggled to put my shoes on while stuffing every book in my vicinity into my backpack, I started unintentionally thinking aloud, "Today is going to be a bad day, indefinitely."

"What are you talking about?" Micky asked. Although his first period English teacher granted him a free excuse from classes that day due to a "sudden occurrence"—which rarely meant a true emergency so much as an unplanned vacation—my roommate, who had no limits to his abnormal habits, still got up at six thirty that day to study grammar for his Italian class.

Realizing I was still more or less asleep and thus unaware of my actions, I glanced back at Micky to reply to him with a frustrated tone, "I've already received another tardy to chalk up to my record. One more, and I get another demerit. I can't stand having these blemishes on my grade report, not to mention an earlier curfew as punishment. To add on to that, I hit my toe on the door when I was rushing to brush my teeth. These are, if anything, bad omens for the day. Stuff like this has happened before and I always got bad grades during those days."

"Aw, you don't honestly believe in all that bull, do you?" Micky asked, "Those were just unlucky events."

"You're unlucky," I said childishly, "I don't want to get into some weird talk about fate and the universe. My teacher's going to flip out at me." I zipped up my backpack and headed out the door, not before accidentally slamming the door against my toe. Fortunately enough, however, my dull brown boots, ridden with residue from mud and slush, shielded some of the impact.

My stomach ached and growled, vying barbarically to greet some innocent bagel, pancake, or even the cold pizza crust slowly growing mold inside the dorm fridge. In spite of that, the instant the cold outdoor air entered my nostrils, I grew attentive and it felt like my senses heightened to a peculiar level of alertness that mimicked some experimental stimulant. The melting icicles loomed frighteningly over the edge of the roof, and the crunch of snow against my boot soles sounded as annoyingly piercing as nails on a chalkboard.

Hallucination was an equally possible candidate for my unexplainable morning agony. I think it helped suppress the anxiety of seeing my aged, traditional first period English teacher, Mr. Woerhy who gave individual grades for every class.

I received a B minus that day, because he mistook Blake Beckett for me, who also had dark hair and a pentagonal face. As far as Woerhy and his grade book were concerned, Blake received an F for entering class tardy without an excuse that day.

Chapter 4

Five minutes before the beginning of history class, I walked into Carter's classroom and saw the malicious teacher sitting at his desk. He had reading glasses on and was looking at the morning newspaper with steaming coffee from the dining hall, which always served watered down, low concentration beverages.

Teachers always had it easy. They only taught a few classes and had the rest of the time free to either grade papers or sleep. Half of them lived for free—including free water and electricity—on campus with their families inside houses that took up half of a dormitory. Carter was on of those people, which only made me detest him even more.

"Here you go," I handed the three wrinkled pieces of paper after history, held together by a paper clip, to Dr. Carter, who I imagined had a vendetta against me for the intrusion into Galloway House fall term. Of course, I never fully perceived the man's face through the blur that night, and so I tried to avoid any presumptions. For all I knew, it could've been Carter's twin that I hadn't met yet.

He kindly received the pile of crinkled mess from me with a falsely genial smile, "I'm surprised to see that you finished it. It was a hefty assignment, no doubt. To be quite honest, I really had no intent for you to complete it, given that, while you are technically speaking still my history student, you're no longer in this particular course."

"What do you mean?" I stammered nervously, with a bewildered smile.

"Therein lies the issue with the effectiveness of school mailboxes. Something should be done about that. No one would consciously and regularly look for mail, who has time for that?" Dr. Carter babbled. I wanted to punch him. "I digress, the fact of the matter is that I merely filed a notice to the administrator, who, in turn, decided that you should be moved down. The course change should be in your mailbox."

If I didn't have a temper issue before, I definitely had a condition then. Never had I seen such outright inappropriate, disdainful fatuousness from a teacher until this point. My other teachers may have been boring, eccentric, or even irrational, but this man took the cake. However, I had enough sense to refrain and hold my tongue. Just a gritting of my teeth and clench of the fist expressed my disapproval of both his words and actions well enough, so I thought.

However, in periods of true shock, I am never able to yell or grit. Often, my anger only completely fills me with true rage long after a conversation has ended, when I am able to contemplate what I wish I could have said in the moment. So instead of having an inappropriate fit that would, in all probability, place me in front of the Disciplinary Committee, I stood awkwardly and noticeably leaned on my right foot.

"I understand your disappointment Mr. Walther. 'Do not be quickly provoked in your spirit, for anger resides in the lap of fools', Ecclesiastes chapter seven, line nine," the irritating teacher prattled on, "I'm not too fantastical about religion, but I'm still a Christian man myself. What about you, Mr. Walther? Are you a man of God?"

"I'm not Christian, sir," I hurried to get back to the point while my anger was at its culmination, "Sir, this isn't—"

"Well? What do you believe in? You do believe in a god, don't you?"

"No sir," I struggled for a short time to get back to my question until ultimately relinquishing to his, "I'm an agnostic atheist. Sir."

"Why's that?" he inquired while still remaining in a calm posture, a facet that I envied. Instead, when put in an uncomfortable situation, I always fidget with my fingers, have a shaking voice, and uncontrollably swallow every couple seconds while worrying that my swallows are loud enough for those around me to hear and viciously judge.

"Well, for one, I just don't believe in a madman who uses infinite power to allow his cult followers to infect subsequent generations with anti-intellectualism," I replied. At this point, my anger had dissipated into perplexity. What had started as the delivery of an assignment had now morphed into a repulsively philosophical tête-à-tête.

"You might be thinking of Jesus. God, whoever He is, constantly watches us. Now, I think some of our interpretations of the Bible have been perverted, causing wars and violence," he continued.

I humored him, as well as myself, "I think He's long abandoned us."

"Nonsense," he replied with a pretentious smile, "He exists in this world as long as we continue to believe in Him. If you're thinking about a giant face popping out of the clouds to talk to us over tea, however, then you're right, that won't happen."

"In that case, then, He's just an idea. God wouldn't let so much evil roam free, and He certainly wouldn't allow a teacher to unjustly move one down a course with little excuse," I felt proud that I had managed to bring the point back from its tangent, but my chest started to pound again out of tense rage.

Dr. Carter looked as if he had more to say, but instead he took a bite from the waxy red apple sitting on his desk. Simultaneously, the bell rang. I asked for a note, but he promised that the teacher wouldn't mind me being a few minutes late.

He was somewhat correct. My teacher let me off with only a stern warning about late arrivals. What perplexed me, though, was that Dr. Carter had somehow managed to divert my fury away from him, and focused it into a conversation about religion. This man, although he may have been the greatest manipulator in the world, seemed like a pretentious, malevolent, worthless piece-of-crap teacher to me.

I gave myself an excuse to avoid walking to the history building. Rather than beginning a disrespectful tirade against my unjust teacher, I went to the mailroom on the other side of campus.

When I went to check my mailbox for the course change slip, I found a tardy notice as well, which read, "9:55—3rd Period Tardy—signed Administrator Hastings". Whoever Hastings was, if I ever met him, I knew I wouldn't like him.

I had little time to contemplate my fury as I sprinted to the lockers to avoid receiving a second tardy notice from my sprightly squash instructor, too. Micky and Big Ed stopped me before I almost ran into them at the ice rink. "It's Tommy boy," Micky exclaimed as he stepped off the ice rink with his skates and heavy padding, "don't you have practice soon?"

"Yeah," I responded while hyperventilating, "I had to go to the mailroom and check my course change. Fucking history teacher moved me back down to history two for no reason. But he's still my teacher. He has some sort of grudge against me, and I don't know exactly why."

Big Ed grunted, "This guy sounds like a douche bag. Sucks to be you." He put his goalie helmet on and stepped back into the rink.

Micky patted my back with his giant glove, "Listen, Tommy boy, it sounds an awful lot like this guy's asking for it. I'm sure Ed would love to throw a nice heap of knuckles into his face."

"That would be nice to watch," I said sarcastically, "but I don't think Big Ed could live with just one punch, though. As much as I hate squash, I don't want to get a demerit for it. I'll see you later." After only two minutes in the ice rink, even with a heavy winter jacket on and an elevated heart rate, I started shivering and my fingertips had begun to lose circulation. My increasingly building indignation, however, seemed to insulate me quite well.

During squash practice, I tried as much as possible to distract myself by engaging in conversation with other bored squash students. The conversation often turned to complaints against teachers and classes. It was tedious, but helped me avoid thinking about the devil that was obviously possessing Dr. Carter. What a bastard.

Only a few minutes after I spaced out looking at my reflection in a glass door, a disruptive vibration hit my eardrums. "I don't mean to disturb your session of self-admiration, but we're up for some squash again."

From my daze, I jerked my head up to the source of the noise, "You again?" For the past weeks of practice, I hadn't seen this blonde girl among the mass of squash participants.

The instructor, out of complete laziness, didn't bother to change my partner up. This time, her safety goggles were removed, and the buzzing, low-hanging lights illuminated her green eyes in her pale face.

"Sorry to disappoint," she replied in a hurry. Without further comment, she headed into the court.

Still caught in my choleric thoughts, I played worse than the first time, barely moving to hit the ball back. After I let six points slip by, the instructor and the girl had grown bored, or at the very least peeved, at the extent of my inactivity. "Are you all right?" They both asked. "I'm fine," I would respond before losing focus again thirteen seconds later.

Only when Elise snapped her fingers in front of me did I finally snap out of my trance. Out of some defensive instinct, I grabbed the hand until it pulled away. "Sorry," I remarked, feeling more proud of my reflexes than embarrassed about seizing her hand.

She gave a scowl before walking off the court rubbing her hand. Now I was embarrassed, yet also slightly intrigued. By then, the clock read fifteen past four, and so I headed off to the locker room, abashedly, with the rest of the glob of people struggling to reach the showers first.

Some people charged through others to snatch a spot, fully clothed, to the best shower. The locker room showers were nothing appealing, though. It often sprayed a spectrum of lukewarm to scolding hot water.

After changing, Micky and Big Ed walked in with the rest of the hockey team, recognizable by the scraping noises of their skates against the concrete floor. Micky approached his locker with heavy metal blades still on his feet, large shoulder pads strapped on, and gloves hanging from his hockey stick. "You know, walking with skates wouldn't be a bad idea in the snow. They cut through snow easier."

"What about walking on top of the snow with giant shoes?" I joked.

"Yeah," Micky pondered as if I had just proposed the greatest invention in history.

"They're called snowshoes," Big Ed pointed out after noticing that Micky had not yet processed the existence of snowshoes.

Micky's face turned red for a second before throwing a stern look at Big Ed, who was laughing for once. "Have you showered yet?" Micky asked, trying to divert the subject.

"No, but I'll do it back at the dorm," I replied.

"Wait," Micky halted, "you're not going to shower now?"

Suddenly, I felt like I was in a bad comedy. "No, because I didn't sweat at all today as usual," I responded curtly.

"That explains the stank," someone commented while passing by my row of lockers. I only caught orange hair in a blur and the blade of an overused hockey stick.

"Who was that?" I asked Micky.

He looked over for a few seconds, squinting his eyes to get a good glimpse. "I got it," Micky slapped his knee, proud of his ability to recognize someone at a distance.

"Well?" I asked in vexation after a long moment of silence.

Micky took a double-take and looked back at me, "What?" he asked in a sincerely imbecilic tone.

"Who was that guy?"

"Oh. I know."

"Thanks, old man," I commented sarcastically at his dementia-like behavior, "Who was that asshole?"

"Well," his voice picking up an undeservingly prideful excitement, "that is none other than the our good and precious co-captain, the only sophomore captain ever to be chosen, Harlow. He's in our grade, you know."

"Most pretentious name and personality, if you ask me," Big Ed mumbled quietly, in order to avoid the echoing in the locker room, while grabbing his towel, "I'm surprised that guy's ego fits inside that tiny head of his. If he's not boasting his nonexistent charm with girls during practice, then he's showing off with some stupid trick. He's in our grade, too, so we have to deal with three years of practice with this bastard."

Micky chuckled and gave a heavy pat on Big Ed's back, which made him exert a gruff groan, "Aw, Ed's just upset he scored on him with an open net today. Coach Carter yelled at him something rough."

"Carter? As in Dr. Carter?" I asked, immediately attentive again.

Micky and Big Ed exchanged suspicious glances for a split second. "Yeah," Micky replied, "why?"

I started pointing at my chest, my hand flopping violently like a fish on dry land, "That's my fucking douche bag history teacher!"

He made an unusual scoffing noise that almost resembled a giggle, "Are you serious? That sucks. I can't believe you didn't see him, he was standing almost right next to us in the rink." His eyes lit up and he gasped, "Oh, man, Tommy boy. If he heard you complaining about him, then you are unquestionably screwed."

"Why didn't you tell me he was your coach?" I asked, clenching my backpack in disquietude.

"You never asked. Why didn't you tell me he was your history teacher?" Micky wondered, attempting to be concerned but, in all actuality, indifferent to my issues.

"You never asked!" I exclaimed in a shrill voice. I still remember that it was shrill specifically at that moment, because my throat hurt for a little while afterwards and forced me to borrow Micky's lozenges, which had melted and grown sticky under the sunlight from the dorm window.

"Listen," Micky said while grabbing his towel, "I'd take this opportunity to switch out if I were you. This could very well be a bad omen. I'm going to go take a shower, wait up for Big Ed and me for dinner."

I looked at him with frustration, "I thought you didn't believe in omens."

"I don't," Micky replied, walking away from me towards the showers, which still had a long line of people waiting to wash off. "But you do."

That night, I sat there, scribbling down what looked more like gobbledygook with each word. My writing was eventually replaced with exasperated thoughts of how the English language was so unnecessarily intricate that the world would be better off just pointing to things rather than talking.

I wasn't completely angry, per se, but more annoyed. Either I was going completely insane, or everyone around me was. "You okay?" Micky asked, apple in hand, "You've been keeping to yourself for a while."

"I've been dealing with all the bull that this school's thrown at me, hoping the good times, as promised, will be delivered to me," I groused apoplectically, "but not even one year into this fucking school, and it's like I've been here for twenty just waiting for a reward."

"That's because you're waiting for a reward," Micky pointed out, as if his psychological prowess had the answer.

Fed up, I shook my head in wild aggravation, "What are you talking about?"

"I don't know," Micky shrugged, "what are you talking about?" As preposterous as he sounded, Micky was oddly insightful, even if I didn't want to admit it.

I had no reason to be angry since all that happened was that the hockey coach was also my abominable former history teacher. I should've been more afraid, if anything, considering that I yelled about him while he stood virtually right next to me.

During the rest of the night, I spent a solid hour staring at my chemistry homework blankly while thinking of ways to get back at Dr. Carter. Right away, I decided that I would stay in the higher history section and completely ignore the course change. Looking back, the plan seemed juvenile.

After finishing my homework that night, I skimmed various parts of a Bible that had been in my desk since the beginning of the year. I had no true understanding of its content. Finally, when my clock read three in the morning, I found the perfect verse. I wrote it down, stapled it to the back of my history sheet.

However ridiculous it seemed, I felt proud of my plan. If I couldn't yell at my teacher, maybe a form of a more muted attack would do him some justice. His absurd discussion of religion was obnoxious, so I'd give him a taste of his own medicine.

The next day, I arrived at class as I did every day, and Dr. Carter didn't say a word about my unwelcome presence. While it was peculiar, I assumed that he had acceded to my confrontational effort. I turned my homework in with a suppressed grin and a raised chin. I was proud of my subtly assertive initiative. I had hoped that he would place my paper into the pile with the other papers. Unfortunately, he noticed the page staped to my homework assignment. He glanced at the words briefly before placing the paper into the pile on his desk.

I was confused by what had happened. But after a while, it hit me, like a bat to a baseball. I had gotten myself into a worse situation than before. "What if I get in trouble for doing that? I mean, nearly half a dorm was expelled just for getting caught smoking marijuana," I worried aloud later that night.

Micky, believing I was expressing my concerns to him, turned around from his desk, but not before taking a bite from his red apple, "How about from now on, it's a given that I never have any idea of what you're talking about unless you tell me exactly what you're whining about."

Struggling to be courteous, I regrettably explained to him the current problem. "I wrote 'An unjust man is an abomination to the just: and he that is upright in the way is abomination to the wicked.' It's a quote from the Bible."

His guffaw, which typically sounded like a cartoon donkey, had an outlandish chirp to it. "That won't get you into trouble, Tommy boy! If anything, you should be mortified that you quoted the bible to Coach Carter!"

"You wouldn't get it. It's a long story," I excused in an attempt to comfort myself from the shame that resulted from Micky's obnoxious laughter.

He was right. What I thought was a a brilliant plan to show Carter that I was well-bred and intellectual was actually childish and pointless. My face flared up in shame, and I could feel the blood rushing to my cheeks. For God's sake, I had written down a bible quote. This school had made me crazy.

Not atypical of other nights, I couldn't sleep during the four hours that I allotted myself that evening. This time, it was not because of work or stress, but my anxiety towards my infantile actions that kept me up and perpetuated my dysfunctional sleep cycle at Kingsley.

Every day since I had arrived, I always managed to pull myself out of bed long enough to turn off my alarm, often unconsciously. That particular morning the next day, it took an entire thirty minutes of painful internal struggle to force me out of bed. What woke me wasn't Micky's raucous closet digging but my own fault of falling onto the floor. When I was little, I had always thought that my intense kicking and thrashing in bed would be my downfall.

A couple minutes before the start of history, I stared at the cold desk in front of me for what almost felt like hours. Dr. Carter left the room when I walked in, and I preferred it that way. Confrontation had never been my strong suit. Luckily, nothing odd happened during class. Historical events about the New World were thrown at me in a barrage of dates and time periods. At the conclusion of class, the teacher handed back the graded assignments from the previous night.

I went through the rest of the day's routines, constantly half expecting Dr. Carter in a monster mask to jump out at me before realizing the ridiculousness of this thought. My brain couldn't make any sense as to why he had not reacted to my paper, not even a discussion to confront my clearly belligerent note. I was almost insulted by his passiveness. Damn, that man was crafty.

Being the inconsolably neurotic wreck that I was, I could do nothing that night but fade in and out between concentration and worry. Paranoid, I rubbed my temples and took out the graded history assignment, which I had not yet looked at, from my worn binder. The paper had an insignificant crease in the top left corner, where the staple was. After a careful examination, it was clear that no writing was anywhere to be seen on the two pieces of paper, but only check marks throughout what I believed was a poorly written history response sheet. The lack of a grade on the paper was disarming and unusual.

At that moment, two small strip of paper, one college-ruled and the other faded yellow, fell out, slipped past the desk, and floated down to the dirty carpet floor. Eventually, I saw the out-of-place strips of paper and picked it up. Due to a cursive handwriting that epitomized the illegibility of all teachers' uniform penmanship, it took me a few seconds before realizing that the strip was my indirectly offensive libel. My quotation was crossed out, and below it, he wrote, "He replied, 'Because you have so little faith. I tell you the truth, if you have faith as small as a mustard seed, you can say to this mountain, 'Move from here to there' and it will move. Nothing will be impossible for you.' Matthew 17:20."

I wasn't sure whether to be confused, relieved, or both. Before deciding on any fixed emotion, I read the "A+" that embellished the back of the paper in green ink. The second yellow strip of paper showed a familiar format of black squares enveloping some lightly printed words, "Teacher Requested Course Change—Thomas Walther—Requested Change: Remove History 2, Add History 3—Signed: Administrator Hastings".

Was it compassion, pity, or respect that compelled him to keep me in his history course? Reading Carter's thoughts was as difficult as writing one of his history papers perfectly; it was impossible.

The instant that my brain registered the course change slip, my determination to remain in third level history dropped considerably. Weighing the pros and cons in my head, I eventually decided that I would find second year history more advantageous to my grade and time. From a logical aspect, I finally saw my situation more clearly, understanding how pointless and time-consuming my perseverance to vindicate myself from Dr. Carter's injustice was.

The next day, I walked to the scheduling offices next to the mailbox room with a request to change to a different teacher. A woman at the desk simply looked up and told me that it was too late into the term. Apparently, I had also received a few unexcused absence marks for attending Carter's class when I didn't belong.

So with the rest of winter dying down in ordinary boredom, the term ended with an odd feeling in my gut. My scores were likely fixed at a B minus, and the growing damp warmth of oncoming spring provided an unidentifiable, mixed aura to my surroundings. I had lived in New England my entire life, but the shift in seasons that year had never felt so dramatic. Micky's chattering felt more unbearable, the final exams felt incomplete, and my departure for spring break felt premature and undeserved.

Upon the completion of finals week, on the last night of winter term, I banged my fist on my desk out of chagrin from reminiscing about recent events. Micky woke up, with a paper glued to his head from the humidity. Sweat provided a reflective light on the back of his neck as he wore an outer layer that consisted of a thick, red wool sweater with indiscernible patterns on it, "What's going on, Tommy boy?"

"Sorry," I unclenched my fist, "Didn't mean to wake you up from your nap."

"You're seriously mistaken, my friend," Micky said as he peeled the paper off from his moist forehead, "I don't take naps. I was simply resting my eyes."

"I believe that. I believe that you couldn't fall asleep because of the giant ball of fur that's hugging you and cooking your skin."

"It was a Christmas present," Micky replied, clearly offended, "Besides, as far as I'm concerned, winter doesn't end until twelve tomorrow morning."

"It is twelve," I responded indifferently.

Micky fell onto his bed and grasped at his alarm clock. He glanced at it for a moment and motioned his fingers around, trying to determine the reading of the clock hands. "Oh. You finally have time to sleep. Why are you still awake, Tommy boy? Isn't it past your bed time anyways?" He joked.

"It's clearly past yours," I replied with my cleverly formed comeback, "I guess I just couldn't sleep."

"While your up then, I have a proposition for you," Micky moved his feet to the foot of his bed and put his bathroom slippers on.

"What?" I asked, excited about potential development from the generally humdrum atmosphere.

"Let's go raid the Clockroom. I bet no one's in there at this time," Micky stupidly offered.

I turned around with disappointment, and half knew that he was joking. "Come on, Tommy boy, it was a joke. You won't get very far without a sense of humor, you know."

"A joke has a punch line, and it's usually funny," I snapped.

After a few minutes of uncomfortable sitting, Micky broke the suffocating sheet of silence with an unusual confession, "To be honest, as much as I know I shouldn't give a shit, the stupid club is something that I want to join."

"Are you serious? I've explained to you multiple times about how retarded the society is. Eventually, you even convinced me how pointless it was. For God sakes, you made me sneak in to that goddamn building to try and steal their clock. Why would you want to join?" I asked in an increasingly loud voice. These mixed emotions were affecting my head as well.

Micky cocked his head forward in undiplomatic persuasion, "I'm not saying that I want to devote all my time to this, but that wouldn't be a bad idea. Every one of those students gets into a good college. Think about it."

"You said it yourself, the society is full of pretentious, egotistical richies!" I exclaimed as I unconsciously stared at a patch of carpet under Micky's chair.

"Okay, first of all, I never said that. Secondly, everyone at this school is a pretentious 'richie'—"

"You said something to that effect," I interrupted sternly, "I just can't fathom your opinions, which are neither here nor there." There was no reason to be upset with him. I understood that clearly then and now, but I felt challenged, as if his sudden interest sparked what was once my own mild interest, which grew into a forest fire of competitive drive.

Maybe it was just the long-term proximity to a single person or just the pressure from grades and parents that drove me to become a cutthroat fiend, but my eagerness to conquer even petty concerns stayed with me for the rest of my life. As I sat there in bed that night, with Micky snoring like a bear, I thought to myself the conceited self-worth that I would gain if I were invited into the Red Clock Order. But, even that sounded spectacular to me.

Every struggling evening, with only a small lamp shedding light on a piece of paper, was to get into a good school. My father, as a child, would always tell me how he earned his job at a medium-sized investment company through a mutual old Harvard classmate, while my mother would set constricting limits on my downtime. The issue was that the universe never compensated me for my efforts.

Even just earning the acceptance letter into Kingsley took more than the blood and sweat than my body's capacity. Without my father's legacy to continue on at the academy, I may have still been stuck in my hometown, wilting away during my heyday.

CHAPTER 5

The following morning, my mother came to pick me up with a red Ford Bronco, a car that my father only used to carry large objects and packages. She brought it, instead of the red Mercedes, in case I had unexpectedly decided to pack my entire closet to bring home.

I brought only a single, large bag. Packing had never been my strong suit. I'd much preferred to simply unpack everything into one location and not move. That's why, whenever I did have to stuff clothes for travelling, I simply took everything from my drawers and threw it into my bag, just in case the opportunity arose where I needed shorts in the winter or a fleece in the summer.

When I arrived home and opened the front door, my dog, Cooper immediately rushed up to me, smelling my hand as if he were acquiring a new scent. Dinner that night felt convivial. The table displayed thick imported Kobe beef filets that my father always bought for special occasions but ended up freezing them for a month until my mother finally convinced him to cook it.

The food that night, however, didn't match the gustatory familiarity of a homemade meal that I remembered. The filet, while juicy, wasn't the slightly burnt and almost crispy style of food that I grew used to as a child, or maybe I just forgot the flavor.

The two weeks break went by slowly, each day getting progressively warmer than the last. Contrary to most people,

I never found spring or summer enjoyable and found more comfort in the fresh snowfall of winter.

I had bad memories from the forced summer camps and clothes drenched in sweat, as a child, from the least bit of activity. None of the warm weather or sun-kissed beaches ever appealed to me. I closed the curtains and turned on the air conditioner whenever possible.

Two days into my break, my parents dragged me to the house at Nantucket, forcing me to remove myself from the bed, no matter how much I tried to explain the necessity for my sleep. Any other time, I would've gladly gone to Nantucket and interact with old friends there, but the undefined gap between winter and summer made me want to squirm about in order to shake off the uncomfortable lukewarm temperature.

In contrast, the feeling of sleeping in a warm bed after a cold day of skiing was much better than hiking pointlessly in a desert with sweat dripping down my back.

On the last day of spring vacation, I sat in the living room of the house with nothing to do. All the island kids had gone back to their local schools well before I did. It was lonely sitting on the couch. Although I enjoyed the respite on the sunny island, I felt that I should've been studying the entire time. It felt irresponsible to even look away from my textbook anymore. I shrugged the feeling off before Kingsley could take its grasp into my vacation.

The silver wind chimes in the backyard pinged rhythmically to a light breeze. The sliding glass door leading to the backyard let in a heavy ray of light, which forced me to squint.

Cooper rested his head on my left leg, and so I tried to remain as still as possible while my father put the bags into the trunk of the tan island car. The car was originally white, but had gathered far too much dust and dirt over the last few years for me to consider its paint a pristine color.

My father had only come for the last weekend that I was here, and he checked his phone every moment at the beach or while biking, in case the company needed him back at the office. Sometimes, even, it felt like he was aching to return to his leather executive chair. Secretly, I told myself to never become obsessed with his work like he was. Oops.

During the last few minutes of official break, in the early morning, I swore to myself that I would make this term count, make it a jumping off point for the rest of my career at Kingsley. In theory, the idea seemed not completely absurd, but I was worried that I might've made a false promise to myself. When I heard my mother open the door to call for my departure, I stood up, with Cooper beginning to hop about; I brushed myself off, and staggered outside with a heavy sigh.

We arrived at the same time as during the beginning of winter term, but this time, the sun was still out and the trees had life in them. Micky greeted me with a slight twitch of his head while he, for once, folded his clothes in a neat pile after unpacking. That night, after picking up my term schedule from the scheduling desk, I sat, as I often did, lying back on my wooden chair. The backrest only rose to the middle of my spine, and so I slid down with my neck resting on the slim edge of the glossy wood in order to rest my eyes. Before the house counselors and proctors instigated lights out, I had already fallen into a heavy nap with my tailbone uncomfortable resting on the wooden seat.

Jerry disrupted my rare moment of serenity when he slammed open the door with Big Ed trailing behind lethargically. I jumped up and stumbled unconsciously. Static flickered and corrupted my vision as a head rush began to exacerbate my dizziness. Finding trouble waking up, I walked about until my right hand latched onto what felt like a round piece of cold metal.

When I fully came about, I saw what appeared to be a pocket watch. Instinctively, I looked inside to check to see both hands diligently pointing to twelve. I stood there until I regained my consciousness. Suddenly, a left hand gripped my arm, which traced back to the grinning face of Micky. A fist promptly hit right under my eye seconds later.

Staggering back, I tripped and landed onto my bed as I supported and rubbed my quickly swelling face. "What the fuck? I'm not a human punching bag," I swore, infuriated.

"Sorry about that," Micky apologized genially while rubbing his pocket watch, "you have mighty strong cheekbones, if it's any consolation."

"Man up," Jerry laughed as he picked up a pencil from Micky's desk and attempted to spin it between his fingers, "it barely hit you."

"It looked more like a tap than a punch," Big Ed added with a gargantuan grin on his face. He either appreciated fights too much or had something against me enough to find pleasure in my pain.

I was mad at Big Ed for smiling while I tried to ameliorate the throbbing on my face with a gentle circular rubbing motion. As I urged myself to get over it by landing onto the bed, which squeaked and creaked from the slightest movement, Jerry and Big Ed started to play football in my tiny room that barely fit two beds and desks, as it were.

Two minutes into my sleep, a loud slamming noise followed by a snap of wood broke my slumber. I jerked up, nearly straining my neck, and pointed to the door with my eyes half shut, "Get out of my room right now."

Big Ed crawled up from the debris of the broken closet door and dusted himself off. Jerry looked over at me in my half daze, "Wow, somebody's cranky. It's not like you have to pay for it. Just make up an excuse and the janitors; they'll get it fixed in no time. It's not like it'd make a huge dent in the schools oversized endowment."

"I don't give a shit that you broke my closet," I groaned, "I want to fucking sleep."

Micky opened his arms and leaned back with a persuasive stance, "Come on Tommy boy, you're talking crazy because you're tired."

"Fuck you, Micky," I babbled before quickly plopping my head back onto the feathery plush of my pillow. The relaxation didn't last long, as I woke up groggy and with a headache in the morning after a dreamless six-hour sleep. I saw the broken closet and remembered Big Ed's fat ass crushing the tiny wood door. I didn't want to deal with it, and as long as the house counselor didn't walk in, I'd be fine. The morning accompanied a thick wind that debased the spring sun, which did little to add warmth.

The few bold enough to withstand the punishment of loud rustling leaves and strong winds of the day sat outside on the campus quad doing homework in the late afternoon. The buildings managed to shield some of the breeze, however, but did not prevent papers from flying across the grass lawn. When gray clouds started to dance about across the sky, the outdoors became devoid of life.

The first day of classes was a nice surprise. The new schedule had moved my history course to first period, out of Carter's malevolent grasp. My new classroom was smaller and dimly lit, with only weak orange lights illuminating the chalk writing on the blackboards.

Wooden desks sat in two compact rows facing the teacher's desk. The room, all in all, felt closer and more hospitable than Carter's. My new teacher, Dr. Wright, walked in and greeted everyone with a kind smile. After placing his briefcase down on the desk, he left the room with his white mug, etched with the school seal, to fetch some hot water for tea.

Seconds later, I heard girlish giggling, that of an obsequious student, which made me want to despise the next person that entered through the classroom doors. It took a few seconds for my brain to register the image, but as odd coincidence would have it, the same blonde girl from winter squash with the tightly wound ponytail walked through those doors. Even worse, she chose to sit in the seat right next to me, even though I had purposely tried to shield myself from catching her attention. Losing twice to her in a foolish sport had been adequately uncomfortable, but interacting with whom I believed to be a teacher's sycophant worsened the situation.

After chatting with a nearby friend for a few moments, she looked to her right and noticed me attempting to hide behind my backpack, "Hey squash partner. It's Thomas, right?" She slightly pressed down the large partition of my empty backpack.

"Elise?" I responded with squinted eyes and a wary smile.

"I didn't realize you were in my grade," she said abruptly.

"I'm not," I replied, "I just moved up a history class. I'm a sophomore."

She cocked her head back in surprise, "Is that possible? I mean, I've heard that for languages and whatnot, but never for a history class."

"I guess I'm special," I joked.

She smiled just as the teacher walked back in with a full cup of tea. Straightaway, students began to joke with the teacher as if they were good friends. Dr. Wright, never sitting down behind his desk, jumped around and waved his hands to emphasize his lesson. Overall, the term's course started with a light-hearted manner, leaving me to wonder where this better, more appreciable half of Kingsley had hid from me for the entire year.

That afternoon, baseball tryouts were held on the varsity field. The competition was tough, but I didn't care much. It just seemed like another class, and I didn't expect to make the cuts for varsity. Two days later, my name was excluded from the final team list, and Micky and I enjoyed the leisure of the halfhearted junior varsity practices.

A few nights later, when I was sitting in solitude in my room with only a pencil and paper as my companions, I chose to take an intermission. I had to leave the room, which was stuffy from the rusty metal heater that couldn't be turned off until late April, according to a memorandum pinned to a bulletin board in the dorm common room.

I stepped outside for a breath of fresh air. Suddenly, unsurprising of New England's weather, snow silently began to drift down and melt upon contact with the asphalt. Slowly, a sleek layer of melted snowflakes ruined the crisp blades of grass attempting to build dew in preparation for the next morning. The snow then instantly turned into rain, forcing me to retreat back to the stale confines of my room.

When I placed my hand on the doorknob of the dorm's entrance, I realized right away that I had left my keys on my bed, where I usually threw all my extra clothes and books on during the day and threw onto the floor before sleeping. For nearly ten minutes, I banged on the slim sliver of glass next to the thick wooden door with no luck.

The excess rain that poured over the gutters of the roof began drenching my dark sport coat. A couple minutes later, Micky came walking down the path to the dorm. He noticed me, waved, and paced mildly towards the door with no umbrella and an apple in his hand.

"Irresponsible for forgetting your keys," he said smugly.

"It's just in the room," I said, "I just needed to step out. It's way too stuffy."

"Really? It feels fine to me," he shrugged.

"Just open the goddamn door," I muttered back.

"Look, Tommy boy," Micky sighed, "You have to stop getting so angry. Your hair's turning gray."

He was right, but my anger wasn't directed toward the cold or forgetting my keys. Micky had been pissing me off, left and right, with his carefree attitude and inexplicable erudition, and I had to pay for it. I had started to hate the kid, but since he was my roommate, there was nothing I could do but try and abide to his folly.

"You're upset about getting punched in the face," Micky nodded reassuringly without doubt.

I sighed in return, "No shit. You hit me for no reason."

"No reason?" Micky scoffed in disbelief with an untiring smile, "It's my precious grandpappy's watch." He threw the pocket watch in the air while the scratched gold surface dimly reflected the fluorescent light with a rusty chain flying behind.

"Yeah, and I was just trying to find something to hang on to when I just woke up. I doubt that piece of shit can even tell time," I teased combatively. "Just throw that piece of crap away."

Micky stood up slowly, stretched his neck, and then picked me up by the collar of my shirt. He walked back to his side of the room, bowed satirically, and used his shoulder to tackle me to the cracking drywall. Coughing, I kneed him in the stomach and threw him down to the floor. I wasn't sure if he was actually angry with me or not, but he irritated me, nevertheless.

After several wild kicks and weak punches, I ended up with my back slammed against the wall, my spine in mild pain, until the creaking door forced the cessation of the match. The tall proctor, who lived alone in the neighboring room just as large as ours, walked in scratching the back of his head while glaring at Micky and me. "What the fuck are you guys doing?" He croaked with phlegm in his voice.

With a white undershirt tinted pink from laundry and dark cotton pajama pants decorated with small Mickey Mouse pictures printed on, it was hard for him to look intimidating. The closet on the right caught the attention of his red, bloodshot eyes. The detritus of painted milky green wood scraps still remained unmoved on the carpet floor. "What the fuck is this, man?" the angry proctor questioned as he pointed at the closet space. His quick fuse manifested his New York Italian blood, but his skinny arms and bony build provided no menacing effect.

"Listen, Adrian, buddy, don't worry about it," Micky said as he opened his arms, and leaned back with his persuasive stance again, "We'll get it fixed."

"No, you listen," Adrian replied, "I would've let your stupid wrestling match in the middle of the night slide by, even though I am running on zero sleep—"

"Hey, so are we," Micky interjected. I turned my head slightly away, disappointed by Micky's poor endeavors at cajolery.

"Shut the fuck up, Micky. You're going to be in deep shit, the both of you," he walked out and gently shut the door behind him.

Micky scoffed and grabbed his toothbrush from his closet, "Nice guy, short temper. He's sure as hell got a mouth on him. He's going to get in some deep shit one day with that."

"Maybe you didn't hear him, Micky," I said while rubbing my forehead vigorously, "We're the ones that are in deep shit."

"I wouldn't worry too much about it," Micky gestured apathetically.

After I fell asleep and opened my eyes again, the clock indicated that it was four in the morning, and my roommate was nowhere to be seen. With no energy to collect a search party, I fell asleep again until twenty minutes after my alarm chirped its obnoxious high pitched ringing. I walked into the bathroom and saw Micky snoring on the tile floor. A couple kicks over the course of four minutes while brushing my teeth did the trick.

"You really couldn't have walked the ten feet to your bedroom?" I gave a good kick to his side for good measure.

"I didn't go unconscious here for nothing, Tommy boy," Micky slurred between yawns, "The tile floor is wicked comfortable. You should try it."

"I'm not buying it," I replied, too tired to deal with his shenanigans.

"Well, I also saw a cockroach in my bed. It was enormous," he admitted.

I stared at him, "You couldn't have said anything, or at least told me?"

He glanced up, "I thought you could find it on your own." It was amazing. Knowing Micky, I'd think that he'd befriend the cockroach instead of cower in fear inside the bathroom. If anything, I'd think that he was drunk the night before.

"You look like you're hung-over, without a drop of alcohol in you. Let's go. Classes start soon," I said while spitting the toothpaste into the porcelain sink while warm water washed it down the drain, clogged with instant noodle remains.

Micky pulled his pocket watch out from under his stomach, "I still have about twenty minutes left." He put the watch into his pocket, pulled in his towel as a pillow, and went back to sleep. He looked like a poorly aged vagabond on the grubby bathroom floor with his pocket watch.

"Fine," I muttered, "I'm not waking you up then."

"Fine by me," Micky shouted as I opened the door to leave, "Turn the light off on your way out. The flickering makes the bathroom feel like a rehab clinic." My roommate was its finest patient.

The moment the bell of fourth period rang, I packed my bags and rushed down the empty stone hallway with a few classmates until long, spindly fingers patted my left shoulder. I turned around to see the gangling figure of the headmaster filling my vision. His dim gray blazer nearly reached his knees, and an oversized white shirt and red polka-dotted tie hung against his bony chest.

"Excuse me, Mr. Walther," he said with a voice much steadier than his physical body, "Could I have a word with you?"

I looked back to see my classmates gone, far down the gray hallway. The magnitude of a student's hunger nearly always defeated patience. With a nod and a meager smile, I walked with the headmaster to his office in the building next door.

An ornate, soft, blue and white carpet released a refreshingly musky odor that gave the small office a homey ambience. Headmaster Fitzgerald sat down behind his dark cherry wood desk and rested his cane on the wall behind him. A large portrait of the school's rotund founder, Oliver Kingsley, sat with colonial attire and a bushy gray beard that contrasted against his bald head. The hawk-like eyes of Kingsley stared sternly down at me and, unlike Fitzgerald, terrorized me.

"I received a form today with your name on it," the frail man said as he shifted some papers around the piles on his desk. The table seemed to barely have the capability to bear the weight of the papers and manila folders.

"It doesn't happen to be an excuse from classes does it?" I joked, and then scoffed at my own absurdity.

He removed his circular glasses and rubbed his forehead. His face was young, but his wrinkles, likely a product of stress, masked his face with age, "Actually, it's about your closet, or more specifically your early morning wrestling match with your roommate."

"Those were two separate occasions, and I didn't break that closet," I retorted, ready to burn all bridges in order to save myself from the ensuing punishment. "Micky, Jerry, and Big Ed were fighting while I was trying to get some sleep. They crashed into the closet door, which was actually very flimsy to begin with."

"No need for the nervousness," Fitzgerald calmly replied, "I knew your father, him being the same grade, you know. He was a good student, and a better person than me. I'm sure the apple didn't fall far from the tree. Usually, the typical disciplinary action for rough-housing past curfew and damage of school property would be a censure and curfew restrictions.

"This time, however, I've decided let you off with an unofficial warning in hopes that this juvenile behavior will not continue. Unfortunately, there's nothing I can do for your roommate, as the Administrator has already signed the censure slip."

Mildly relieved, I sighed, "Thank you, sir. It won't happen again." Then, after a brief pause, I ventured, "So what about Micky?"

"Your friend Micky," he said while dropping tealeaves into a cup of hot water, "will, at the least, receive the signed censure and have a restricted curfew. Although, I've had to sign a number of forms for his constantly late dorm sign in times, so it's up to the administrator to make the final decision."

Embarrassed enough about the meeting overall, I left without anymore questions. Back in the dorm after dinner, I decided to remain quiet and not tell Micky about my special excuse from punishment, regardless of how much I wanted to gloat the over my exclusive connections, or more specifically my father's connections.

Micky barged in seconds later, much later past curfew than usual, with a trance on his face that made him appear possessed. He had a shaking grin as he plopped his tattered dark green backpack near his desk, away from its typical spot on the bed. "Hey, did anyone talk to you today?" I snapped him out of his trance with my curious query.

"Well sure," he glanced over before sitting down at his desk, "I talked to a bunch of people today. Did anyone talk to you?"

"No," I scoffed slightly annoyed, "I mean did any teacher or something pull you aside to talk to you?"

"No, did someone talk to you?"

"No, I was just wondering," I tried to recover, rather awkwardly. "Did you get a slip about a censure or something?"

"No," Micky replied, giving me a momentary feeling of disappointment and puzzlement, "but I got a probation letter. I missed curfew too many times, and so I guess the big guys in the disciplinary committee are pretty pissed off at me. I definitely know that the house counselor is because either his love for cake has turned his face red, or he was seething with suppressed rage. Why, what'd you get?"

"Uh, I got a censure," I lied, instantly overcome with guilt for hiding the truth from him.

"Lucky you," he said as he took out the pocket watch from the right pocket of his pants before looking down at my calves. "Isn't it still a little cold for shorts? This year's winter came a little late, and it's ending late too."

"Trying to stay optimistic," I quickly answered. "Aren't you a little happy for someone who just got a probation?"

His repressed smile turned into a full-faced grin and effeminate giggle. Micky looked at me from head to toe multiple times, analyzing me with judging eyes. "No, I can't tell you," he decided at the last moment, with a voice noticeably eager to profess his classified secret to someone.

"I won't tell. I've been locking myself in this goddamn room for this entire term just so my grade point average can go up a tenth of a point by the end of the year, I've got no one to tell," I said.

"Okay," he eventually yielded, trying to appear composed and nonchalant, "I just got head from this girl."

"What? No way," I smiled back in awesome disbelief, "Who?"

"Heather Kelly," he said, "she's a freshman, but she's the same age as us, some starting kindergarten late bullshit."

"Sounds hot," I remarked with condescending approval. "But I'm confused. At most, I've seen you just chat with a girl, and suddenly this freshman shows up?"

"Well where do you think I've been every night for the last couple of weeks?"

"I don't know," I shrugged, "the same place you disappear off to every night practically since I met you, I suppose. Where do you go, exactly?"

Micky waved off my question, "I was off trying to wow this girl. After a little bit of studying with her in the library, it turned into making out in the corner. She's a pretty big slut, this girl, I think you'd have a shot with her, too, if you left this cave of a room." He started to sound smug as he leaned and rocked in his creaking chair.

"Christ, Micky, you're starting to sound full of it," I retorted in defense. I felt remorseful about how intensely my work interfered with everything, but that was nothing new.

"You're just jealous," Micky said egotistically. I closed and rubbed my eyes as I readied myself for my work, waiting to torture me. When would I even find the time to spend with a girl, or even just sleep? It was agonizing, listening to Micky brag about his own conquest.

Fortunately, I completed my evening's assignments much earlier than I had in the small black notebook where I penciled down explicit times for my work schedule. Either it was because teachers had become more lackadaisical with their assignments as summer approached or because I had adapted better to boarding school life, but I had managed to perform more efficiently with each passing day.

CHAPTER 6

As summer crept its way into the year, balmy skies and bright green grass taunted every student glancing outside lustfully. It meant nothing, knowing that I wouldn't be able to enjoy it. The option of studying on the lawn was always available, but I found it inefficient and distracting with other students around, wind blowing the paper, and students tossing Frisbees around.

In the afternoon, the golden sunlight forced my eyes shut during class. The morning, however, was generally enjoyable. I would always wake up around dawn, just in time to greet the sun peering in through my dorm room window. Sadly, I couldn't enjoy it for long if I wanted to make my classes.

Fortune shined upon me one particular morning when Dr. Wright decided to cancel history class. At the time, I was oblivious, but the teacher had apparently assigned the class group research papers on the specifics of the triangle trade in the Atlantic. Only after Elise approached Micky and me on the relatively long path to Commons and finally informed me did I learn of this project. "Hey," she said as she walked towards us, "when do you want to meet for the research?"

"What?" I asked quizzically.

"For the research paper."

"What? What research paper?"

"The research paper that Dr. Wright's been talking about all term. The same one that Dr. Wright gave us class off today for," she replied with a mild annoyed tinge to her voice.

"What? I didn't hear that," I stated, completely off guard by this news.

"Well, besides the fact that he'd been talking about this project the entire term, he also assigned us our partners at the end of class yesterday. Did you really not hear?" she asked.

"No," I exclaimed, "Who can possibly listen, let alone remember, what the teacher says after the bell rings? It's almost never anything important. All I recall is that we didn't have class this morning."

"Wow, you need some better ears," she chuckled. "The pairs were assigned by seating arrangements, so it's you and me, partner. I was going to see when you wanted to meet yesterday, but you left in a hurry."

"Great," I said, trying to withhold any underlying sarcasm. Elise was allegedly the best student in Wright's class, and likely one of the teacher's favorites for her ability to suck up. With short contemplation, I decided that she would be advantageous for boosting my grade with minimal work involved. "Great!" I enthusiastically repeated.

Serendipity had never been on my side, but given the free cut from history and opportunity for an easy "A" today, I thought that maybe luck had finally arrived for me.

"Do you want to meet in the library later at around eight?" she asked.

"Sounds good," I said gladly.

"Great," she smiled as she slowly walked backwards towards her dorm, "I'll see you later. Bye Micky."

"See ya," Micky and I said simultaneously. Micky returned my puzzled stare at him with a friendly smile.

"You know her?" I whispered quietly.

"Of course."

"How? She's a grade above us."

"How, what?'

"How do you know her?"

"I don't know."

"How do you not know?" I blurted out, still in a whispering voice.

"I'm sorry, I wasn't aware that we were supposed to remember how we knew everyone," Micky replied. "It's equally surprising that you know this girl."

"I'm in her class, retard," I responded in defense.

Micky scoffed. "Sure, whatever," he turned his gaze and started staring at Elise as she walked away. "Elise sure has a great ass, though." While perverted comments were not unusual, Micky's level of inappropriateness had grown substantially since he reached third base with the freshman girl a couple weeks ago.

I looked back at Micky with a stern glare as we started walking towards Commons. With his eyes still set on Elise, he ignored me completely, and so I also looked back towards her to confirm his sightline. However obnoxious Micky's arrogance with girls had become, there was no denying the truth in his comment. With a sigh, I admitted, "She does have a great ass."

Looking at her walk away, I instantly realized that she finally had her blonde hair down, out of a ponytail, as well as a sundress on. During dinner, I found it difficult to stop thinking about Elise. I hadn't noticed it before, probably due to my underlying hatred for teacher bootlickers, but Elise was an exceptionally attractive girl.

There was very little conversation while we ate undercooked potatoes and roast beef with mostly fat meat. I could only wonder what Micky was wondering about, and I hoped that he didn't share the same thoughts as me.

Unfortunately, I was not so lucky. "I'm going to go for it," Micky announced randomly while taking a bite from his apple shortly after he had returned to the dorm at night.

"What?" I yelped, startled by the sudden noise.

"Her, to be specific. I'm going to go for her."

What are you talking about?" I asked, already with a clue of what he was about to say. In my mind, I begged to God, any god, that my roommate was not about to say what I hoped. Sadly, He doesn't work that way, especially not the Christian one.

"Jesus, Tommy boy. Do I have to spell it out for you?" Micky said with a smile on his face, "I'm going to hook up with her. What do you think?"

"First of all, she's a grade above us. Secondly, I doubt she'd even want to, you arrogant bastard," I replied in a wild attempt to find ways to dissuade my lecherous roommate.

Micky waved my remark away, "Ah, who asked you, anyways?"

"You did, Micky," I said presumptuously.

With a scoff, the dialogue ended, with the rest of the night coated in silence. The idea of Micky's overconfident idea coming to fruition was nearly unbearable. I had to do something; as absurd as it seemed, I had to get this girl, as if I didn't already have impossible challenges placed in front of me.

The last two weeks of classes went poorly, to say the least. Every time when Elise and I began searching for useable topics for the project, Micky greeted us loudly in the library as if he had no idea we would be there.

For the time being, a salacious, pompous asshole had replaced my once exuberant, slightly obtuse roommate. "So?" Jerry said after I explained the situation to him and Big Ed, "I stare at girls' asses all the time."

"No," I replied, "You don't understand, it's like overly excessive to the point where it's embarrassing. I'm surprised he hasn't gotten in trouble yet for some sort of sexual harassment. Whenever he's near a girl, he starts hitting on them and doesn't stop staring at them as they walk away. It's weird."

"Sounds about right," Big Ed chuckled, "The big man's been full of himself ever since he got head from that girl. She wasn't bad looking either. I say just let him be, he'll get over himself soon."

"Lucky son of a bitch," Jerry remarked, "I don't understand why any girl would want to hook up with Micky anyways, that lazy asshole."

Micky flung open the door with a green apple in his hand. "What's up, guys," he sat down, took a bite from the apple, and quickly spit it out into the full wastebasket near Jerry's desk, "Fuck, these green apples are disgusting. Commons was out of the normal ones today."

Nobody said a word. Jerry looked away, and Big Ed returned to his work. Micky inspected each one of us carefully and laughed uncomfortably, "Why are you guys so quiet?"

"Micky, dude—," I started.

Big Ed picked up his backpack and put in on his desk, "Listen guys, I have to get to work."

"You're a buzz kill, Ed," Micky said as Big Ed shooed us out of his room.

"You," I said as I motioned Micky to his chair, "are completely full of yourself. It's starting to piss all of us off."

"What?" Micky started vigorously fidgeting with his pocket watch, "What do you mean?"

"You always act pretentious," I spat. "Plus, you pretty much hit on all of these girls."

"Whoa, I'm loving the aggression," Micky smirked with a snide response, "You aren't exactly the perfect prude guy, yourself, either."

"Micky," I exhaled, "You're so blatant with your ogling that you may as well be slapping the ass of every single girl in your sightline." I felt out of place for having such an uncomfortable conversation, except it was necessary if I was to stand another second with him.

He nodded back with comprehension, "I know what this is about. Yeah, you're worried that she's starting to like me. It's okay Tommy boy, I'll let you have her." I could see his fingers crossed behind him.

"For fuck's sake," I burst out, "You are so egotistical, and there's no way in hell that she would hook up with you."

"We'll see about that," Micky winked and set his pocket watch down.

After my roommate left the room, I crumpled a piece of paper and furiously threw it to the ground as it gently met the carpet floor.

Eventually, I convinced Elise to change locations in the library, albeit to a location farther away from the research books but unbeknownst to Micky for a little while.

"Why does Micky keep trying to find us?" she asked spontaneously as we had just begun to write out the report.

"I don't know," I lied, "He's starting to like himself a little too much. How do you know him?"

She struggled to find her words, "I was his tour guide when he was visiting for his interview here. He was pretty shy," she replied.

I laughed for what felt like five minutes. When I finally wiped off the cheerful tears that built up in my eyes, I sniffled and looked back at Elise, who had a confused smile on her face. "That is too rich."

"What's so funny?" she asked with a mildly nervous giggle.

"Nothing, nothing," I waved, "What do you think about him? He's crazy, right?"

"I don't know," she shrugged as she pulled on the end of her skirt, "he seems nice." Her blonde hair dangled, and the tips rested on the table in front of her, I noticed that much, but I could only concentrate on how enraged I was with Micky for no definite reason.

So spring term of sophomore year ended with little adventure. For the project, Elise and I received a full grade for the report, but I only earned a "B" for my standalone presentation while she earned a full grade for hers. To be frank, talking in front of an attentive class had never been my suit to begin with.

Confidence was my greatest possession, and so I was not a wealthy man. My grades in the end were only slightly better than winter term's, but I gave myself a congratulatory pat on the back for the job half done. Micky, near the end of the year, seemed to have given up Elise, and his head had mostly cleared of his pretentiousness.

According to a friend, he had heard that the boys' dorm nearest to the center of campus had only open spots for two-student rooms, of which there were many. He proposed rooming again next year for a definite chance at the dorm.

With some hesitation, I ultimately decided that the location and the comfort of the large prospective building would outweigh the suffering of Micky's shenanigans. We filled out the housing forms and turned it in to the dean of residential life, who glared at us as she accepted it with a compassionless smile.

"What was wrong with that woman?" Micky asked as he scratched the back of his neck.

"Bad day, lot of papers to look at, I guess," I replied while staring down at the marble tiles of the Thomas Jefferson Hall floors.

"So, Tommy boy, what are you doing this summer. Not more work, I hope," he slapped my back with an amicable intention, but it still stung for a few seconds afterwards.

"I'm going with my parents to Nantucket."

"Well, I'm going to my family's beach house for a month in a private island in the Bahamas. If you ever stop by, there are a lot of girls my age, and I know a guy that sells some medical grade sativa, real top notch chronic."

"Jesus Christ," I laughed with shockingly no frustration at Micky, "Where did these undiscovered facets of yours come from?"

"I have no idea what you're talking about," he replied. At least his brain was just as dense as it was on the first day of school.

I didn't care. The long three-month summer vacation, a relief from the scheduled school days, would assist in alleviating all the stress of Kingsley. Of course, there was no true break for me during any of the four years of high school.

I had, in secrecy with my father and his connections with the president of a large investment-banking corporation, a plan to attend an unofficial internship to wow the hard-to-please college admissions officers.

"Are you just going to stare at the sun on some beach?" Micky scoffed as he kicked a pebble.

"Yeah, probably," I muttered, starting to feel bad for lying. "Aren't you planning on doing the same?"

"Well, yeah, but I'll probably be high the whole time," he retorted. I scoffed and grinned. I had always had a curiosity for marijuana—such a common boarding school drug—but the magnitude at which students took the drug made me hesitant to ever try it. An opportunity was always there; half of the kids in Connecticut loved to smoke joints every day.

That was the last time I spoke to Micky before he left for his flight home. I didn't return to the dorm until after dark and spent my limited free time with dorm mates in downtown Windham. Some of the stores in the area never closed due to the large number of Kingsley students who wandered the area at all hours of the day.

We spent a large part of the evening at the small, family-owned coffee shop, the most popular venue for students.

I relished those few hours, because I knew that the moment I stepped into my mother's car tomorrow morning for the long trip home, there would be no opportunity for jubilation.

On the first day of my internship, I sat on a black leather couch with my mother in the middle of the large office of the company's president. With the acoustics of the large room, every small movement echoed with the creasing noise of leather. After ten minutes of waiting and staring blankly into space, a tall, dark-haired man walked in with a clean black suit.

The man introduced himself as Mr. Whitaker, a senior vice president at Morgan Stanley who would allow me to shadow him for the next five weeks. At first, I felt out of place in the cold, air-conditioned office as my mother chatted up the businessman for nearly half an hour. After she left, though, I learned that the man was unusually friendly, far from the corporation archetype that I had imagined, but I couldn't say the same for others around me.

Other workers stared at me judgmentally as if I didn't belong, and I didn't.

For the remainder of the morning, I stared at a photocopied report of a small, unknown, miscellaneous company. Half the document contained only numbers with terms that I didn't understand. It quickly made me ache for a nap.

At lunchtime, I had finished "reading" the report, and Mr. Whitaker invited me to go to a business lunch with a colleague. Hesitantly, I nodded and joined him to a fancy restaurant where patrons raised their pinkies while lifting the glasses of soda water they drank to momentarily quell their desire to drink at noon.

The stuffy conversation was friendly in appearance, but I could tell that it was all fake just so I wouldn't complain to the president of the company. It's as if they believed I was a small child, although I wasn't much younger than some college interns.

The internship, overall, was nothing too difficult, as long as I didn't mind killing time in an empty cubicle throughout the day. The commute from Connecticut to New York, however, did cause some frustration. It took an hour-long train ride from Connecticut to New York City, and then a very expensive cab ride from Grand Central Station to the office building every day.

Sometimes, I would sneak out of the building early just so I could return home and sleep. If I didn't nap at home, I'd have probably napped in the office, anyways. In the mornings at home, I found any excuse not to leave on time. If I had any sort of responsibility that would let me contribute to the company, then perhaps I would not have found going to work so dull.

At the end of the five-week venture, my mother forced me to give a fountain pen to the president of the company as a present. Instead, I gave it to Mr. Whitaker, with whom I found was friendlier. The president, whose name I never learned, didn't even bother to actually meet me, ergo I didn't bother to thank him.

For the rest of the summer, I stayed with my parents at Nantucket, occasionally going swimming or biking. However, I almost never did much more than sit around in the house and enjoy a nap while inducing cabin fever. Before I knew it, the summer ended almost uneventfully.

Whenever an adult asked me about my highlights at the internship, which they viewed as impressive, I would hide the fact that it was boring and napping became routine. I simply explained that it was "enriching" to have been submerged in a "dynamic, powerful workplace of a company like Morgan Stanley." But work was never meant to be fun. The only thing "enriching" would be the money that came in from hard work and fixed fees.

Kingsley always set aside the first day of school for orientation. When new students with thrilled smiles and nervous, shaking hands walked into Jefferson to register, I couldn't help but smile proudly and scoff mentally. I knew that I was one of those people last year, but these new freshmen and sophomores looked almost pathetic and contemptible.

A heavy smack on the back welcomed me to Micky's presence as he held an eager smile similar to that of the new students. "Hiya, Tommy boy," he yelled out, trying to speak above the clamorous crowd.

"Hey, Micky, how've you been?" I asked professionally. After not seeing my roommate for three months, any anger towards him was automatically, but temporarily, replaced with wholehearted merriment.

"I've been great," he flung his hands out, nearly hitting my face in the process. "I've been eating more lettuce lately to stay healthy. That's a thing, right?"

"Eating lettuce to stay healthy? I . . . I guess," I stammered. "Well it's good to know that you're trying to be healthy for once."

Relieved that Micky didn't try to investigate the activities of my summer, I suggested that we head to Commons to eat lunch. Later that afternoon, Micky and I headed back to Jefferson to attend returning student registration. Instead of innocent, naïve faces, the students in this horde had smiling faces with mild anguish and scarring underneath. It's possible, though, that I may have misinterpreted them.

At the front of the mass of people, I waited as a stern, paunchy woman sat indolently at her desk moving papers around. "Thomas Walther," I repeated a few times loudly to make sure she heard.

"I know," she exhaled nasally, "I heard you the first time. Just wait while I get your papers." It was clear why it took two hours to end up at the front desk. The clean tile floors and marble walls contained the air-conditioned room. Inside it, the chubby woman with a sweat-filled towel around her neck sat in a low, blue chair behind a large desk shared with two other people.

Immediately, her temper was discernible, but I couldn't care less as long as my new school year papers ended up in my hands. After some waiting, I finally received a white envelope, slightly torn at its edge. I took out the papers inside and opened it up.

Along with my dorm keys was a thick piece of paper that detailed my schedule.

Micky looked over at my paper as he held his in hand, "Hey, you have Fitzgerald as your advisor. I heard that guy's pretty nice for an uptight headmaster." The occurrence seemed coincidental, but not extraordinarily bizarre.

As Micky and I headed out to check out the new dorm room, my past and current roommate sparked a moment of keenness and noticed Elise from halfway across the crowd. I was less concerned, albeit still slightly uneasy, with any future attempts of Micky flirting with her, given the fact that he was a young, sheepish freshman with Elise as her tour guide not even two years ago.

Turning away from her conversation with a friend to address Micky's nonsensical yelping from across the room, Elise looked over at us and smiled enthusiastically, "Hey guys. How were your summers?"

"Great," Micky jumped in before I could even process her question. "You look pretty good." He glanced down at her dress.

Stunned by Micky's quick response, she glanced at both of us. "Good, thanks," she stuttered. "Do you guys have your new schedules yet?"

"Yeah," Micky continued.

"Maybe you could stop by some time," I jumped in audaciously with little contemplation before Micky could resume.

"Yeah, maybe I will," she bit her lower lip as she kept gave shifted glances to the both of us.

We said goodbye soon and headed over to the new dorm, which was a quick thirty-second walk. The new room was, itself, divided into two small separate rooms. Micky quickly called the one in the back, joking that he would probably get more action with girls and require it more often. Waving off his pesky sense of humor, I sat down on the squeaky bed and fell asleep for a short while.

When I woke up, I found Micky sitting at his desk, eating an apple and playing with his pocket watch. He was unpacked, and his entire room was already organized as if he had lived here all year. "Where the fuck did all this come from?" I yawned.

"What are you talking about?" he asked in response.

"Don't play this game," I said crankily, "How did you get all your stuff here. I was only asleep for an hour or two."

He shrugged, "I had some help."

"From who?" I wondered. To the extent of my knowledge, he and I didn't know anyone living in the dorm at that point so far.

"Coach Carter," he said. Right away, my heart sunk and my head filled with a sour anger. "He's our house counselor."

"What?" I exclaimed.

"Dude, it said on your schedule."

"I didn't read it completely. I hate that guy, now I have to fucking live with him?"

"Watch your language," Micky scolded. Worst of all, class hadn't even begun yet and this despicable man, who called himself a teacher, walked into my own room while I was drooling and asleep on my bare bed.

Aside from the distraught information, it felt great to be at school, yet not have any work for a day. There was still, however, a feeling of unproductiveness that made me yearn for some task to perform out of boredom. After lugging all my boxes and bags from the basement of my old dorm to the new one, there was really little to do. I did, however, feel more mature than last year, bolder even.

At night, the two house counselors, Dr. James Carter and Mr. Tilder Gerald, came by all the dorm rooms to call a meeting for all the students in the dorm. Luckily for me, Gerald, a fifty-year-old math teacher, managed my side of the dorm. He had graying, curly hair and a thick mustache. Like Micky, Mr. Gerald had an affinity for referring to students as "boy," effectively creating a pretentious, cowboy-like demeanor.

For the first few days, I referred to the man as "Dr. Gerald" before realizing that he had no doctorate. His tough, introverted attitude prevented him from correcting me. I didn't like him, but he still was outstanding compared to Carter.

"Ah, Mr. Walther, good to see you. I was beginning to worry that you might never wake up," Dr. Carter smiled as he raised his head from a clipboard with copies of the dorm sign-in sheets. He removed his gold-rimmed, square-framed glasses and inhaled deeply. "Welcome to the new year, everyone," he bellowed in the high-ceiling common room.

Students looked over at him from the uniform couches and tables, "I know some of you, but not all of you, and we can change that. Feel free to talk to Mr. Gerald or me if you have any questions, particularly the new students." Mr. Gerald had clearly been overpowered by the formidable upstaging of Dr. Carter's aggressiveness. The more Carter talked, however, the more he tested my fuse. His lifeless staring and muted sarcasm muffled the false hospitality in his inane speech. It took all my strength to not stand up and punch him in the face, but I could tell that he knew that. Fresh chocolate cookies soon filled the air of the packed room as Mr. Gerald's wife brought out tray after tray of small baked desserts for us. The meeting ended with content students, who were uneager to return to learning.

Regardless of our disdainful attitude towards homework, no one functioned properly at Kingsley without some assignment from a teacher. It just didn't feel right. It was as if the teachers had some clever plot to make students crave work right before school started. For me, their devilish plan had worked, and I embraced the first day of work that my teachers gave me, although I partially expected a single day of just talking in class. After all, no instructor enjoyed teaching immediately after summer.

For the week, little events occurred. By some miraculous chance, I made varsity soccer, but only as a placeholder to fill the roster. I enjoyed the games, solely because I could sit down and doze off while clumsy high school students kicked a ball of air around on a grassy field. The heavy rain during practices made soccer all the more exciting, as well.

I remained with the same history teacher, Dr. Wright, as last year, with the same blonde girl, now a senior, sitting next to me in the exact same classroom. "Your hair's shorter," I remarked on the first day of classes while she was in the middle of taking her books out.

"Yeah," she smiled, "I got a few haircuts over the course of three months, you know."

"Well it looks good," I recovered. Embarrassed, I looked down at my desk. Months of inactivity and studying at my desk last year may have hindered some of my social ability, if I had any.

Choosing boldness over a reserved security, I started making an effort to be around Elise more that term. Before a test, I would always invite her to study in the library or at the dorm before a history test or quiz while her friends around her stared at me, the younger student, disdainfully.

On a Saturday before an important history test, I invited her to my dorm to study, except the common room door was locked. "Great, there's nowhere to go now. It's not like the library's open at eight on a Saturday night."

"How about we just study in your room," I looked over at her instantly, but didn't see a trace of anything unusual.

"I guess," I shrugged after realizing I hadn't moved or spoken for more than a few seconds.

After knocking on the door in inconsistent rhythms for a minute, a dorm mate down the hall glanced over as he searched for the keys to his room. "Mr. Gerald's gone. He's giving a late test," he looked over at Elise and smiled, "talk to Dr. Carter about parietals." He opened the door and closed it shut behind him.

I closed my eyes and swore under my breath with a heavy exhale. "I love Dr. Carter. I had him for history freshman year. He's really nice," Elise said, evidently growing somewhat impatient.

"Are you sure we're thinking of the same person here?" I scoffed, "maybe I've been talking to the long lost evil twin."

"Come on, let's go ask him," she motioned over.

I never liked Dr. Carter's wing of the dorm. He controlled four floors, although his house took up nearly half of it, a generously larger ration than Mr. Gerald's home. She knocked on the door, unbearably ardent, to talk to him.

He opened the door, dressed in professional attire even in his own home on a Saturday afternoon. "Ms. Poitier," he said cheerfully after glaring at me for a moment, "what an unexpected surprise, pleasant, nonetheless. How may I help you?"

She pointed over at me, "Parietals, if it's all right with you?"

He dissembled his impertinent attitude and traded it with condescending comments, "Intriguing, I didn't expect

Mr. Walther as a parietals kind of man. Just remember to keep the door open."

"Don't worry," she smiled politely and walked briskly down the hall with her books in hand.

"Could I speak to you for a second, Mr. Walther? Please, step into my office, if you will," he said. Intimidated, I looked over at Elise, who had already found my room even though she had never seen it before. I slowly stepped into his room.

The large office was well lit, but the orange glow of the lights made the space seem deceptively dark. Aside from trinkets and tchotchkes sitting on the tables under packed bookshelves, the room was relatively bare, with little amusements or distractions.

"Would you care for a drink?" he pointed over at a bottle of whiskey sitting in a locked cabinet.

"You can't be serious, sir," I chuckled uncomfortably as I stared at the bottle with skepticism. It wasn't, however, the first time I had tried whiskey. Between my father and I, liquor was the only thing we had in common since I turned thirteen. I never appreciated the taste, but sharing a bottle was the only way I could earn time with the man I considered a paternal figure. My mother, a sober woman, had no way in with her husband, though.

He smiled faintly, "Of course not. I was just kidding around. At least we know you're not an alcoholic."

"So, what was it you wanted to talk to me about?" I couldn't think of anything subtle and viciously insulting to use against Dr. Carter.

Dr. Carter sat down slowly into his executive style leather swivel chair, "Take a seat, I don't plan on taking much of your time."

Hesitantly, I sat down in a painfully rigid wooden chair. Its intricate, edged carvings poked into my back, and the dust from the nearby table put me on the verge of sneezing.

"I hope you and Ms. Poitier aren't planning on doing anything that would require the request of a disciplinary committee," Dr. Carter closed a drawer full of pencils lined up neatly in stacked rows.

"No," I replied abruptly, "just studying."

"If you are and you get caught, and I will catch you if you are, then a disciplinary committee will take such actions seriously," I could tell that he was toying with me and just wasting my time.

"You know what?" the chair moved back and put an uneven fold in the carpet as I stood up suddenly in a rage that was barely sustained, "you keep trying to sabotage me or something every chance you get, and without reason. And also, I know that it was you walking out of Galloway with the rest of those pretentious kids in the Red Clock society, which doesn't do anything except judge everyone while its members sit around and drink tea."

He started chuckling pretentiously while I hyperventilated in front of his desk, "Your depiction of the Red Clock Order is quite imaginative."

He remained sitting and gazed up at me without moving his head, "You know, your father and I were in the society together. Has he told you, yet?"

"I don't know," I responded, somewhat dumfounded and more exasperated now than enraged, "my parents and I aren't close enough for me to have known that. I don't really talk to him."

"That's a shame," he looked down at his desk and shifted some cards and papers around, "I never spoke to him much more than I needed to, anyways, but it's best if I make sure you stay out of trouble. But just for your information, it's best if you don't have any more room visits with your friend. I was also in the society with Mr. Poitier, and I knew him much better. You are dismissed."

The anger returned, yet all I could focus on was how tired my feet were from the two minutes of standing. I left, slammed the door behind me, and stormed down the hallway. I heard laughter upon entering my room, where Micky and Elise seemed to be getting along too well.

"Hey," she said jovially as she saw me walk in.

"I think that I should study alone, I could probably concentrate better that way," I said pensively.

"What are you talking about?" she asked as she walked away from the doorway to Micky's room.

"Yeah, what are you talking about, Tommy boy?" Micky added. I glared over at him.

"I haven't been doing too well in Mr. Wright's class, and I guess that just means that I need to change up my study habits," I replied.

"No way, it's become a tradition. We'll just study twice as hard, is all."

"Tommy boy? Studying? Nonsense?" Micky interrupted again.

"All right," I agreed, "well there has to be somewhere we can go without distractions."

"I know," she grabbed my arm and pulled me forcefully until her hand slipped down to my wrist. It felt cold and warm at the same time. Normally, I would've been happy considering that I hadn't had time for a good friendship with anyone in the past year aside from the obligatory one established with my roommate, but I could only think about Dr. Carter's abhorrent face and reprehensible behavior.

CHAPTER 7

A few hours later when I entered the dorm again, I noticed Micky's name already on the sign in sheet. "Hey, how's Tommy boy?" he asked as he spun around to face me at the room door.

"Well this is a nice surprise," I remarked lightheartedly, "You're never in the dorm before I come back."

"That's a bunch of hokum. So tell me, did you get lucky with this chick?" he asked childishly.

"What?" I stood back aghast, "We just studied."

"Are you telling me that you just spent the last three hours reading a history book?"

"Pretty much."

He scoffed and turned his head in disappointment, "I don't get you, Tommy boy. Your adventures are a real mystery to me."

"Look who's talking. Why are you suddenly so supportive? Given up?" I looked over suspiciously.

"You wish," Micky laughed, "don't worry about it, Tommy boy. I'm going to bed. Preseason for hockey starts early tomorrow morning."

"Fine," I replied quietly. Something had definitely got into him, and I was hoping that it wasn't bipolar disorder. Micky, aside from his eccentricity often mistaken for magnanimity, had never been a credible person, let alone a reliable friend.

After a grueling three months of work, Christmas break nearly caught me by surprise. When I sighed and set down my pencil, I didn't expect to see a Christmas tree, gingerbread house, and overall cheery atmosphere—all the fixings of a typical Christmas—waiting for me as I turned around. Ice-cold rain began the three-week vacation until snow finally took its place.

Micky and I, on the last day of school, walked to breakfast with no rush and a load of pressure off our shoulders. "What are you doing over the break?" I asked Micky as I stared down at my visible breath in the cold air on the walk back.

"Believe it or not," Micky responded, "I'm having trouble figuring out the answer to that question, myself. My parents, as much as I love them, were actually ignorant enough to forget to tell me that they have to travel to visit my sick grandma. I, for sure, don't want to go to that."

Upset at his disrespect for his family, I stopped and fully turned to face him. "Why wouldn't you want to visit your sick grandmother? I'd bet a hundred bucks that she'd visit you if you were sick."

He chuckled with a relaxed composure. "You clearly don't know my granny then, Tommy boy. She's a bitter old woman who hates everyone, but has somehow still survived a million diseases that I've never heard of," he opened his hand out and grinned, "now pay up. You just lost the bet."

I shook his hand and smirked back, "A good handshake is worth a hundred bucks."

"What a surprise, Tommy boy," Micky replied in jovial bewilderment, "that's the first joke I've ever heard you make this term."

We had reached the dorm and saw my mother's car a metallic red Mercedes double-parked in a space nearby. She stepped out as soon as we neared the area.

"Hello son," she said with a hug, "and good to see you Micky. I hope you're packed, Thomas."

"Good to see you, too, mom," I acknowledged, "I am packed, but I didn't realize you were coming here in the morning."

"Well, of course, dear," she replied with a frown, "I called you on the dormitory telephone many times to tell you. Don't you remember?" Her forehead wrinkles were well defined, a feature that I believed that I would develop by the time I graduated.

I remembered. I remembered that I didn't listen to a word she said but rather placed the phone on the table, occasionally giving grunts of confirmation.

"Of course," I said. "Well, my things are all ready in my room."

She nodded and sighed, but immediately shifted to a pleasant face, "Do you have any plans for the holidays, Micky?"

"Actually," he glanced over at me as he straightened his back and lost his childish manner, "I was just talking to Thomas about this. I actually don't. Something came up with my parents, and so I am without any plans until Christmas Eve."

"Nonsense," my mother waved, "You can join Thomas and us in Whistler at our mountain lodge. I presume you can ski?"

"Absolutely," Micky nodded, "but I don't want to impose."

"Of course not," my mother courteously replied.

"Okay, I'll just call my parents. Thank you so much, Mrs. Walther."

I chuckled softly, having never seen Micky speak in such a prim and proper manner. For the longest time, I thought I was the only one our age who could be so fake. Still, it wasn't unusual for a person's personality to change in the conscious presence of an adult, but I expected Micky to be rather static in his ways.

When the sunless sky started to cool the air's temperature, much of my family, except for my occupied father, drove up to the lodge at Whistler. Having not visited the large, isolated resort for a few years, I spent a few minutes letting the scent of piney cinnamon fill my nostrils. The elevated ceilings and high loft were difficult to adjust to after spending so much time at the low ceilings of Kingsley dormitories.

My bedroom had gathered dust from the time I didn't visit. Occasionally, the lodge was rented out, and some of the furniture had been shifted around. Micky stayed in my room, in the other bed where my noisy, young cousin often slept in on these family ski trips.

That night, we went to rent a pair of skis for Micky before going to dinner at a restaurant downhill from the lodge. The house was relatively isolated, and the walk was quite far to the rental facility. I looked at my watch—something I only wore on rare occasions—to make sure that dinner wouldn't impede too much on my studying. We returned to the house at approximately ten o'clock, which was frustratingly late.

Instead of enjoying the hot cocoa and refreshing mountain air, I spent all my time before Christmas indoors studying ahead and absorbing small portions of textbook drivel up indoors. As the snow layered onto itself, burying and suffocating all the grass and plants, I started to feel my tension entombed as well. "What have I become?" I questioned myself aloud while I sat alone in my room, "Kingsley's going to be the death of me."

On the last few days at the lodge, I had hit the wall and reached my studying maximum. However, when I finally threw my books down and hoped to ski down the mogul steeps, I received a phone call from my mother at the infirmary near the bottom of the mountain. "Thomas, I think you should come down here," she told me anxiously.

"What happened?" I asked as worriment began to speed up my heartbeat.

She paused for a few seconds and sighed, "I think you should come down to see for yourself."

After asking the concierge multiple times for directions, I found my way to a small building with its lights aglow through the windows.

When I walked in, a pudgy receptionist sat with horn-rimmed glasses and was looking down at some paperwork. She looked up at me with an eyebrow raised, and quickly looked back down without a word. "Someone called and told me to come over," I stated.

"Sign in on the sheet on the table," she responded with an angry inflection. There was no table.

"I'm not sick," I responded.

She glared up at me, "Sign in. On the table."

"There's no table, ma'am," I whispered. Honestly, out of every menacing person I've met, this rotund receptionist was the most intimidating. Perhaps it was the outright rudeness, something that I had only ever experienced from others with their subtle mask of niceties.

She looked around, sighed sharply, and plopped the book on the dividing counter in front of her. "So," I slurred, "Why am I here?"

She glared up at me again. "Upstairs. I'm not in charge of the patients." Clearly she wasn't in charge of anything, especially not portion control.

With wild searching and a reluctance to ask help from the fat lady, I eventually found the small door that led to the stairwell. Upstairs, the flowery walls and medicinal stench gave me thoughts of just leaving the floor at once. In order to return to my work as soon as possible, though, I walked into the only lit room with an open door and saw a nurse working diligently at her desk.

"Are you Thomas Walther?" she asked with friendly character as soon as I stepped in.

"Yes," I replied with a squint. The bright light burned my eyes as I tried to adjust from the dark hallway. "Am I in some sort of medical trouble?" I asked.

"No," she chuckled, "not exactly. Just go down the hallway and into the last door on the right."

"Why?"

She smiled and looked at me over her glasses, "Your friend has had an accident."

Timorously, I took small steps until I finally reached the room with the lights on and what sounded like plastic clinking together. My mother first came out and shut the door behind her, "There you are, Thomas."

Upon seeing that she was okay, I felt a wave of relief, "What happened? Is someone hurt?"

"Just go inside and find him," she pointed at the door.

"Come in," a familiar voice called after I knocked on the door a few times.

With the sight of the entity in front of me, I leaned back and nearly smacked my hand to my forehead in astonishment. "Hey, Tommy boy!" Micky shouted, with apple bits and spittle flying out from his mouth.

My puzzlement faded when I saw a leg capsulated in a bright, white cast. The fluorescent lights suddenly looked yellow in comparison to the clean bandage wrapped around

Micky's calf and ankle. I stared at it and back to Micky for a few seconds with wonder.

"I understand your concern," he said while taking a new apple and kept eating without discontinuity, "so I was skiing through some trees, and then I decided to ski backwards."

"So you hit a tree, and your leg took the kill?" I attempted to finish the story for him.

He motioned for me to settle down, "I made it through the trees alive, barely, until some incompetent snowboarder rammed into me. Can you believe that? Skis are hard as hell to get out when they're stuck inside a mound of snow." He chuckled, "Well, at least I didn't pop out from my skis and go flying down the hill."

"You okay?"

"Aside from the minor fracture, I'm okay. I could walk if I wanted to," he moved to the edge of his bed while trying to hide his wincing.

"That's not such a good idea," I remarked, not bothering to try and help him. I knew it'd be futile to stop the obdurate Micky from changing his mind, however harmful it was to him.

Luckily, a nurse came in to check on Micky and found him almost putting weight on his broken fibula. She rushed over and nearly tackled him off the other side of the bed, "For the seventh time, you're not allowed to put any weight on your leg whatsoever," she glared over at me with scorn. "While you visit, it's your responsibility to watch him as well, Mr. Walther."

"I was planning on using my crutches, anyways," he fibbed as he winked at me.

"Sure you were," she replied with skepticism.

He took a bite from his apple and then spit it out with disgust, "Could you bring some better apples? The ones you have here are too waxy for my taste."

"Those are the only ones we have," she responded cantankerously before pacing back down the hallway.

"Terrible service, these nurses," Micky joked.

"So, I'm guessing that skiing is out of the question for you?" I asked.

"Yeah, well, it's not too bad. There's plenty of food and television. Besides the fact that this place looks like a mental facility, I'll manage. There's only a couple days left, anyways," he said with a grin on his face.

My mother walked back in. "Michael, I haven't been able to reach your parents, but I'll try again later. We should let Michael find some time to rest, dear, I'm sure he'll need it after today's fiasco."

"Well," I sighed, "I was going to go skiing, but after this stressful surprise, I guess that's out of the question."

"You can go skiing if you want, don't let me hold you down, bud. You've been holed up inside your room for the past few days when you've been missing out on some perfectly good snow. It's fine by me."

"It's not fine with me," my mother retorted, "Your friend is hurt, Thomas, you can't go off skiing while he sits all alone. It's unacceptable." The conversation was futile, anyways, because the next day, precautionary avalanche measures were taken due to a heavy blizzard. As a result, the entire mountain closed down until the morning that we had to leave.

Regrettably, I spent most of my day visiting Micky upon his request. By the end of the week, on the last night, he was released from the hospital with crutches and a pack of painkillers, something he should never be around. "I'm feeling a little woozy, Tommy boy," he garbled as I helped him reach the snowmobile that would take him back to the lodge, which was an otherwise long walk uphill.

With only one seat for a passenger, I walked back to the lodge from the infirmary for the fourth time that week. Micky arrived before me, and I found him snoring with only his lower half actually on the bed.

I decided to leave him there, not out of anger but out of pitiable commiseration. Sleep was a necessity that prioritized above any interruption. An hour later, he woke up from his heavy nap to take more pain relievers to cure the agony of a painful leg. He struggled to hop over to his chair and rest his cast on top of his desk. After some time, Micky realized my confused expression. "What?" he asked, "I have to elevate my foot so my blood can circulate."

"You're insane," I laughed with some admiration to his commitment.

"Never mind that," he garbled as the painkillers started to take noticeable effect, "It's too bad that you couldn't ski, Tommy boy. It was some be-eeeautiful snow out there. There's a time and place for everything, though, Tommy boy, and Christmas vacation is definitely not the time for work."

"I know," I replied with sorrow as I sat down on his bed, "Too bad I didn't realize that until the avalanche came down."

"It's all right," he assured, "There's always next year."

"Yeah," I said softly. I knew, though, that there would be no time to pursue any hobby if I were to commit my time to look at colleges and begin my applications. Still, I just nodded in false agreement.

"By the way," his eyes batted from languish, "how's that Elise project going for you?"

"What?"

"You heard me," he said, coughing a little.

"I don't know," I responded, "I thought you were after her."

He shrugged, "That's on hold for now."

"I don't understand," I responded, "your change in attitude doesn't make sense. Weren't you the one that arrogantly decided that you would go after her with indefinite success?"

"I'm over that," he dismissed with prideful aplomb.

Being the foolish child I was, I simply laughed at his response stupidly and thought nothing of it, again. What drew my attention more was what I heard next. "Listen, Tommy boy, I've never asked you for a favor the entire time I've known you, right?"

"I, I-I guess," I stammered and shrugged without much thought.

"Well, I have one that I need from you now," he requested.

"What is it?" it sounded serious, given the grave tone in Micky's voice.

"You can't let your mom tell my parents, or let anyone tell my parents for that matter."

"Why not?" I asked, caught off guard by his sudden intensity.

"You're a good kid, Tommy boy, but you need to open your eyes a bit," he snapped, "they're not off visiting my grandmother, although she is a pretty bitter woman, and I wouldn't visit her anyways."

"Where are they?"

"They're off in Florida enjoying their time on the beach. They think I'm at home right now doing absolutely nothing except sitting on my ass, which was my original plan to begin with."

"Wow, your parents didn't want to bring you on their vacation? That's a little insensitive, isn't it?"

"No," he chuckled, "it's nothing like that. They implored me to join them, incessantly, I might add. But the truth is, and I love my parents as much as I'm supposed to, but they are just too much to handle. Half the time, it feels like they're just pretending to care, I feel like I'm on some cruel television show where God is the director, and the rest of the world is in on it."

I didn't speak but only looked down at my feet. "You can't tell my parents," he requested with begging eyes, "if they found out that I was here going skiing without them, they'd be devastated. Then, after that devastation would come an irate reprimanding regarding my irresponsibility."

"Why didn't you tell me this sooner?" I asked him. It was shocking to see a small tear from Micky's upbeat personality.

He answered, "I'm telling you now, aren't I?"

"Yeah, but this would've been easier if you had informed of this a while ago."

Micky looked away for a second, "Listen, Tommy boy, I was planning on telling you the first day, but I fell asleep after dinner. And then, I was going to tell you somewhere on the mountains while skiing, but you weren't present for that." he replied.

"Just tell your parents," I offered, "At most, you'd probably take a little bit of yelling or disappointed sighing."

"Just do this one thing for me, bud," he pleaded. Normally, I wouldn't have done something so off-putting and unusual, but there was something about Micky's abrupt change in attitude. Until now, I had only seen him as a kid with a single dimension, which originally consisted only of an inappropriate disposition and a flair for the sarcastic. I comprehended his thoughts well, as I felt the same way about my parents, often. He and I, maybe, weren't so different.

I sighed again and pat his back as I stood up to leave the room. On the way to find my mother, I couldn't help but find some humor in Micky's concern.

It took a few minutes to find my mother in the enormous family lodge. She was downstairs drinking champagne and having a comfortable, quiet discussion with her siblings in front of the crackling fireplace. My younger cousins chased each other around with toys in hand while tripping on the carpet every now and then, much to the obliviousness of their parents.

When I asked to speak to her in private, she gave a disturbed glance but quickly adjusted into what she considered to be a motherly face. In reality, I could see the ghostly eyes behind the dim smile and raised cheeks that she thought amicable.

Maybe it was because of her emotionless care that I remained distant to my parents since youth, or maybe it was out of my distance that her detachment was born. Both of my parents always approached me with the same demeanor, and I had never loved it when they did. I had thought nothing of it until Micky mentioned his own distant relationship with his parents. Before that, I only went through the hugs and the holidays as if they were my inherent duties as a son, particularly an only child.

Aside the dim fire, I lied to my mother and told her that I had already reached Micky's parents and explained everything. My mother professed that she regretted not speaking personally with his mother but was glad I accomplished the task.

When I had returned to the bedroom, Micky had fallen asleep again, this time on his desk with his pocket watch in hand, and a lamp lit in the corner. As I studied the strong oaky scent that the loft often emitted, I laughed quietly every time my friend snored in uneven intervals. Up to that day, I had no clue of Micky's other sides. Like me, he hid behind multiple coatings of grins and impenetrable lies. The only difference was that he played the part better than me, showed more commitment.

The blizzard subsided the morning after, and we drove down the mountain for the long haul back home while Micky slept with his foot up in the backseat. Two days before Christmas, my mother and I sent Micky to the train station for his ride back home. He wavered with his crutches as he spoke, "I'll see you in a few days when school starts again, Tommy boy."

"Yeah," I squinted from the sunlight's invasive angle, "Don't take too many painkillers. Have a Merry Christmas, buddy." He nodded and smiled before hobbling away. From the back, his faltering steps and his shroud of falsified lightheartedness displayed what I had, for years, wondered in myself. I knew there was something off about him when he entered the dorm for the first time sophomore year. He was conceited in the same way that I was malevolent, and neither of us showed it. Still, in the likeness, I felt some antipathy for myself and for him.

CHAPTER 8

The typical heavy New England snow arrived late that year, and so the only indications of wintertime were the dry air and thick overcast. Micky said very little on the first few days back at school, which allowed me to return to the normal routine of studying, sleeping, and eating. Jerry and Big Ed were the first few to sign Micky's cast, but in a single school day, he ended up with his entire leg covered in colorful signatures. The bottom of his cast had become brown from dirt and his toes blue from the cold air and sockless foot.

On the morning of the first Friday, my advisor, Headmaster Fitzgerald, reached out to his six students personally and announced an advisory meeting—the first one that year—during the school's office hours, a thirty minute time slot every morning used for discussing work with teachers but was often misused for napping in the library. The six of us that were gathered in his office were from different ages and all had different, distinct interests.

I was one of two juniors. The other one, an unknown student named Eric, had slick, brown hair and sat quietly with his hands in his lap. He was in my English class and often sat in the corner with his book in hand, laughing with everyone else at jokes but otherwise sulked passively behind his desk. So with nothing in common except perplexity at the absence of Fitzgerald, we sat in the stagnant musk and awaited the arrival of the Headmaster.

Five minutes in, Dr. Fitzgerald entered and apologized for his tardiness. He then decided to speak with each one of us individually to discuss our progress at Kingsley in alphabetical order. As misfortune would have it, I was the last on the list. I sat back down in his office right when the bell was about to ring. He didn't speak for a few moments, but then looked up with his thick glasses and smiled warmly. "You've been doing well this year, so far."

"I'm sorry, sir?" I asked, slightly dumbstruck from the compliment, something that I hadn't heard since before my grandmother passed. The effects of Fitzgerald's remark were so strong that I could nearly taste it. It tasted sweet, like the guts of a golden brown marshmallow in a cold forest. It's not that I hadn't heard a single compliment for years, but I hadn't heard any that had any meaning in them.

"Your grades," he continued, "they're one of the best in your class. I'm guessing you're a modest kid, Thomas. I know you might not believe in your ability as much as you should, and I don't want to induce any sort of overly prideful behavior, but they are very good. Don't lose your determination, and no more troublemaking. I don't mean to keep you from your classes, though. Have a good day."

"Thank you, sir," I said with a smile. Maybe the stress paid off, and all the work had finally come to fruition. Nevertheless, I kept trying to tell myself that even more devotion to studying was necessary.

I walked to my third period with a grin on my face that I couldn't get rid of until my teacher informed me of my lateness. The day ended, though, on a good note.

It took only a few days until disturbance paid its regular visit into my room again. "Tommy boy," Micky mumbled as he struggled to walk in with crutches and an apple clinging by the stem to his mouth.

I jumped from the noise he made in his graceless attempt to open the door. "Jesus, Micky, you scared the shit out of me."

He dropped the apple onto his desk carefully and rapidly spun around. "Hide your porn, hide your cigarettes. Coach Carter's coming! I nearly ran into him trying to beat him to our room."

"I don't have any of that," I replied monotonously.

"You can lie to me all you want, buddy, but that won't hold up in court when Carter comes to arrest you," he clumsily organized his desk and threw some unwanted boxes under his bed. "He's nice when he's happy, but gets mean when he's angry. Like, he gets really mean. The other day, he nearly knocked one of Big Ed's tooth out with a puck for letting in a goal after waving at some girls during practice. I swear, the guy's face turned red and everything."

My unwavering determination to withstand Carter's bullshit fell the moment his sharp glare and stringy, receding hair entered the room. Something about him made me want to punch him and cower in fear at the same time. He smiled and acknowledged Micky, asked about his leg in a formal but polite manner, and then asked to speak with me. My frustration toward Carter seemed ephemeral, as fear replaced all emotion when I followed him down the hallway.

The man didn't say a word until I stepped into his office, and he closed the door behind him. With any luck, I wouldn't have to say anything back. I slithered into the fragile wooden seat that I had become familiar with from the last meeting. Dr. Carter sat down behind his desk, which seemed to contain the same amount of papers since fall term.

"I assume you know what this is about?" he inquired, deadpan.

"No. Sir. I don't, sir."

"Oh? I had thought you'd have heard," he exhaled in a manner that I assumed was representative of a shrug, "you can relax, Mr. Walther. Your tenseness is conspicuous."

I had no idea how to relieve such an emotion, and so I simply forced my shoulders down more and slouched my spine into a minor arch.

"Mr. Walther, at the beginning of every winter and spring term, I like to check on the students that I oversee in the dormitory. It's become less of a requirement from the school, and more of just a personal habit. I'm sure your advisor has done the same, though in less detail."

"Oh," I said softly, "Yes, last Friday."

He nodded. I hoped for an influx of appraise and good thoughts, but knowing my spiteful relationship with this demonic incarnate, I knew that I couldn't expect the same words as those from the headmaster. I was right.

"Well, your grades have improved. You're doing better in history class, I see," I couldn't determine the emotion in his tone, and so I just sat there bobbing my head to every other sentence.

After having a stuffy discussion about progress, my future at Kingsley, etc., Carter handed me a few pieces of paper with comments from teachers of each of my courses last term. "You have a respectable future, so long as you work for it. There's no such thing as studying too hard."

I wasn't sure if he was trying to slip an insult under his words, but I smiled and received the paper kindly. "Thank you, Dr. Carter. How's the Red Clock Order," I asked slyly out of some poor impulse. The moment the words slipped out, I regretted it.

"Good," he replied out of reflex while looking down at his desk. Upon realizing what I had asked, he glared back up at me. His straight face turned into a frown. "Explain to me this, Mr. Walther. The most important thing in a secret society is given in the name. Secrecy. Yet on what I could only assume is a personal vendetta for one night when you were beaten down by a student, you seem to have this odd fetish for corrupting the single organization that pays for this school. Of course, by some inexplicable coincidence, you have caught my attention."

"I don't understand, sir," I replied. I could tell my voice was reaching a higher pitch, as it often did in nervousness, "I didn't do anything wrong."

"Have a good day," he picked up the newspaper lying on his desk and began reading it. After a moment, he looked over at my perplexed face, "You may leave, Mr. Walther."

I found my way back to my room on the other side of the building. Micky was sitting there with a blank stare and a small rectangular note in his hand, which he quickly hid into his desk when he saw me. "Hey, Tommy boy," he greeted with the largest grin I'd seen on Micky yet, "what'd Coach Carter want to talk to you about?"

"I don't know, exactly. He talked about my progress, whatever that means. I don't think he really gave a shit," I complained, "isn't Mr. Gerald supposed to do that? Since when did Carter care about our half of the dorm, anyways?"

Micky shifted unsteadily in his chair, which made stuttering creaks under his weight. He paused and looked down in contemplation before shrugging it off nonchalantly, "I don't know, I guess he just likes us."

"Yeah," I chuckled, "Obviously. Did he talk to you yet?"

"Yesterday," he replied concisely.

With a heavy sigh, I sat down in my wooden chair with poor lumbar support. I studied my teachers' comments diligently. As I flipped to the next page, a small, thick piece of paper fell onto the carpet. The paper was coarse, possessed the school seal in blue on its front, and had some writing in dark red on the back.

It took a few moments to process, but I eventually understood it was an invitation scheduled in the middle of February to a private club dinner in the Bishop Room, a capacious space, which was often locked, located at the center of Wilkens Commons. At the bottom of the note were instructions that emphasized the importance of this meeting's confidentiality. If I wasn't so sure that this had correlation to Dr. Carter and the Red Clock Order, then I would've assumed this was some intricate plot for a mass kidnapping.

Instantly, though, I realized that Micky possessed a paper of a similar size, but I didn't get a good look at its details. Instead of trying to confirm Micky's note and risk my own invitation, I chose to remain silent. My first opinion was reluctance, which would quickly change if Micky was invited, as well.

I'd always liked winter as my favorite season, but that year really took the cake. My teachers were nice, my grades were acceptable, and best of all, I thought that my least favorite adult at Kingsley had finally grown an approval of me.

Of course, I wasn't so foolish as to assume that ecstasy was permanent. I knew that all good things were fleeting, especially for someone as inconsistent as I was. That night, I slept like a baby, only to wake up five hours later to my endlessly obnoxious alarm.

In the course of three weeks, after the meeting with Fitzgerald, I had spent plenty of time meeting with the lanky headmaster during office hours. I think what drew me to those conversations were the craving to be in the presence of his genuine friendliness, a rare attribute at Kingsley.

At times, I questioned if I should've sacrificed so many opportunities to study in order to speak with him. But given his familiarity with my parents, I convinced myself that it was a duty to do so. Fitzgerald was constantly late, but I often discussed my classes and teachers while he shared anecdotes of his time at school.

Eventually, I told him about my invitation to the "club meeting." I explained to him my difficulties with Dr. Carter as well. He later confessed his hidden knowledge about the society. "It's my duty as the headmaster to know about these things," he told me. Although there was some suspicion as to whether or not he was an assisting faculty liked Carter, I learned that he wasn't part of the society but just a bystander of it, according to him.

"I won't tell anyone, but you cannot speak of this to another soul," he advised, "if you want to have a chance at acceptance, then you'd better keep your mouth shut about this invitation."

"It's okay," I assured him lightheartedly, "I don't really want to join this secret society, however interesting people claim it to be."

"Why not?" Fitzgerald asked, both stunned and offended. People took the club far too seriously.

I looked down at his desk as I fiddled with a small, loose chip on the chair's armrest, "the idea of an elitist club within a school that already flaunts its exclusivity is just preposterous. Furthermore, I'd have to attend all these meetings to be a part of a group that I can't even talk about."

"Listen," he tried to explain softly. I could sense the severity of what he was about to say in his tone, "this school, while prestigious, is still just a school. The struggles and rewards leave you the moment you graduate, and you end up with nothing but memories, however fond they are. The Red Clock Order, though, sticks with you for life. You will do well on your own, I can see that in both your personality and your grades, but the society can help you do better. What you do here will pave the way for the rest of your life, it's not just about getting into colleges through connections; it's so much more."

His passion and interest intrigued me. Unfortunately, the bell rang immediately after Dr. Fitzgerald's convincing speech. His words did give me something to think about, though. The more I contemplated his words, the better the Red Clock Order sounded.

After all, my only motivation for persevering through Kingsley was so I could lay out a respectable future for myself. So I spent the few hours of my sleep lying in conscious contemplation.

"So," Micky asked after dinner the next night, "are you going to ask anyone to the Winter Ball?" To me, it was just another event that could sap time away from my work. Secretly, I thought that the school planned these dances and gatherings to filter out the good students from the bad, the careful from the careless.

"Why? Are you interested?" I joked in reply.

"Seriously, though. Are you?" He asked in laughter.

"When is it?"

"Soon. Middle of February," he responded, "it's on the twelfth, I think."

My eyes widened in surprise. It was the same day as the club dinner. "No," I replied as calmly as I could, "I don't think I'm going to ask anyone. I don't really want to go."

Micky stared at me quizzically, "Why not?"

"Are you going?" I asked defensively.

"Look at me," he pointed down at his leg, "The best I could do is hobble around goofily. I doubt anyone would be willing to go with a cripple like me. You, however, are perfectly healthy, Tommy Boy. Why wouldn't you go?" He was lucky to use the excuse against me.

My mind grasped blindly for excuses, avoiding the truth that I wanted to attend the dinner that Micky was likely a part of as well. Well, how good can a dance called the 'Winter Ball' in February be anyways? It's barely winter. Besides, I doubt that any good looking girls haven't already been asked."

"Okay, Tommy boy, you sound ridiculous. There's a reason that it's an upperclassmen dance only. People get down and dirty. You have to go. What about that Elise girl?" he answered almost instinctively.

"I don't get you," I scoffed, "tell me why you've been so encouraging about Elise lately. Last year, you were so annoyingly competitive."

"I don't know. I'm just over her, I have a short attention span anyways," he shrugged. Perhaps it was Micky's invisible charisma or my own denial, but I chose to believe him, again.

I told him that I'd think about it if she wasn't already asked. "You'd better hurry," Micky advised, "If she isn't already going with someone already, a cute senior girl like her won't be there for much longer." Whatever honest concern Micky had, I think we both knew about the club dinner and Micky was probably trying to find ways to dissuade me. I grew an inch of mistrust towards my roommate again, but it was nothing to make me hate him, yet. Knowing Micky, he'd find a way to make me despise him more.

In preparation for the last history test of the year, excluding the final exam, Elise practically invited herself to my dorm out of routine. We sat in the common room and spent half the Sunday studying diligently and only occasionally asking for help when necessary.

After studying every corner of the review, our intensity and focus started to gradually wane. We began to just talk, discussing everything from Dr. Wright's hilarious eccentricity to old stories during kindergarten. Elise eventually asked, "Are you going to that Winter Ball?" Jesus, why did everyone have to know?

"I don't know," I replied casually, "I'm not sure if I want to go this year.

"Why not?"

I shrugged and stared down at the wooden patterns of the large common room table in front of us, "I really don't know. Too much work maybe."

"That's a terrible excuse," she laughed playfully.

I smiled back but remained relatively emotionless. "Are you going?" I asked just to make conversation.

She looked away, "I've been asked a few times, but I just told them I was already going with someone else."

"Really," I looked over in interest, "who?"

Suddenly her extrovert attitude sank into a moment of passivity, "Well, I was hoping to convince you."

"Oh," I replied quietly. I really wanted to ask her. In fact, I spent the entire time debating the worth of doing so. The truth, though, was that I couldn't sacrifice this opportunity, which was very essential to my future, just to spend a single night with this girl.

For what felt like minutes but was actually seconds, I battled myself over the next few words. "I'm sorry," I apologized sincerely, "I really am, but I can't go. I want to explain, but I just can't."

Awkwardly, I gathered my books in the next few uncomfortable seconds. I stood up and slowly walked back to my room with my head down, with much hesitation to keep walking. I didn't hear any movement in the hallway until I had gotten back to my room. Fuck my life.

Nervous about any confrontation, I stayed inside my room with the door shut for the next two hours studying until Micky came back from dinner. I jumped in my seat when I heard spontaneous knocking, which I would have ordinarily anticipated from loud footsteps entering the room. "How's it going, Tommy boy?" He walked into my cramped room and hopped onto my bed.

"Dude," I said, glad to find someone to share my story with, "Elise wanted me to go with her, and I said no."

He looked at me with more anger than surprise, "What the hell is wrong with you, Tommy boy?"

"Why do you care so much?"

He sighed in exasperation, "When are you ever going to have an older girl, a good looking one at that, want to hook up with you?"

"Jesus, Micky," I laughed in mild panic, "I don't think she wanted to do anything except go to the dance, anyways."

Micky was practically suffocating in seething irritation, "What do you think people do at this dance?" He was practically yelling. "Nobody goes just to fucking stand around for an hour and shake around like an idiot."

Micky stormed out into his room with his crutches. He'd improved with his single-leg walking and could now hobble nearly at running speed. His anger, though, was unusual and extremely rare. I couldn't tell if he was envious or just excessively supportive of my romantic life.

Still, I listened to his words for the next few hours. Behind her competitive, almost cocky exterior, Elise was a pretty, fair blonde. Somehow, however, I thought that my situation should've been predicted. Not even a good day was good for me. Maybe I was just being pessimistic, but cautiousness never hurt anybody.

What was once a pleasant, upbeat morning class, first period history became stale and uncomfortable to attend on the cloudy Monday. I didn't say a word in class, not to the teacher or to Elise. She sat quietly and composedly, but didn't look as disturbed as I believed I did.

I felt bad for saying no, but worst of all, I felt terrible for being caught between two good things, which eventually turned into a rock and a hard place. In reality, it wasn't a big deal, but it just felt so unfair at the time, as if someone in the divine beyond wanted to see me suffer. Maybe it was God.

Out of remorse, I convinced myself that the dinner would conclude well before the dance, and so I took the risk to talk to Elise. When I asked her, she informed me that she had already decided to go with someone else. Her tone was regretful but not completely genuine.

"Shit, Tommy boy," Micky commented after I told him that night, "You really missed the ball on that one. What did I tell ya? You gotta listen to me next time." His pressured anger had clearly mollified into his original relaxed poise.

"I know," I said to myself.

As Friday evening crept along, I prepared myself to attend this mysterious dinner. I had no idea of the number of attendees or even a single person that would be attending, except for my roommate.

Micky was nowhere to be seen that night, however. My guess was that he was either off hitting on some girls or getting ready as well. I put on my blue blazer and my nicest tie. With some minor adjustments to my attire, I headed out the door in anxiousness.

The Bishop Room was, in a single word, extravagant. A brilliant glass chandelier hung from the high ceilings, which portrayed a painting of angels. Each wall held an individual mural of a different seasonal landscape. Several rows of tables were laid out with fine china plates, a profligate accessory only broken out during special events such as alumni lunches or graduation day.

Cater waiters welcomed me, asked me for my invitation, and brought me to a seat with the oaky scent of a new chair. The table had clean white sheets over it, and the silverware had ornate carvings. Slowly, more seats began to fill when I saw Micky walk in. He saw me, grinned, and winked as a waiter escorted him over to his seat in the table behind me.

There were eighteen of us total that filled two rows while the one in front remained empty, and we all sat facing a wooden podium. I knew almost all of the people; they were all juniors and had some outstanding mark either as a great student or a spectacular athlete. Nearly all of them were well known legacies.

The kid sitting next to me was Matthew MacAllen, supposedly the best lacrosse player in school who lived in New Canaan, Connecticut. His father was a Kingsley and Princeton alumni and was one of those way-up-there executives for a successful company, the name of which I couldn't remember.

After speaking with him for a couple minutes, I realized he wasn't the pompous asshole who I assumed everyone else in the room was, given that my first encounter with the Red Clock Order involved me getting punched by someone who was, in fact, a legitimate pompous asshole.

Soon after everyone settled in, the waiters quickly brought out bowls of New England clam chowder. Because everyone was so prudent as to not make a wrong move, it took a few minutes before people began eating. The room softened to low echoes of conversation as clinking of forks, knives, and plates filled the large room.

After soup came salads and, finally, generously cut fourteen-ounce filet mignons with asparagus and mashed potatoes. It was delectable, and I could only imagine what slosh Commons had served that night for everyone else. If being a part of the secret society would mean steaks for dinner every night, then there would be no complaints from me.

Two minutes into the savory meal—something that was difficult to find at Kingsley—an elderly man walked up behind the podium. He introduced himself as David Herman. His thick, curly hair was graying and losing luster. The man's forehead wrinkles and crow's feet were noticeable, results of hard work and stress. He was only in his mid-forties, yet he looked much more aged.

Herman seemed confident and successful. He talked about his life after Kingsley, how he made his way through Ivy League schools and a myriad of successful companies until he finally became the CEO of a profitable international services company. I'm guessing he would hope that we would all be amazed and shocked into awe. I didn't find bragging very impressive, but this man probably hungered for praise as much as I did.

Constantly, in measured and calculated words, he attributed his opulence to Kingsley and beneficial "connections from old Kingsley classmates." We all knew he was referring to the Red Clock Order, but maintaining at least a slight sense of concealment was necessary to consider it a "secret" society. He ended his speech with an emotionless "Thank you."

Gradually, the applause died down. We were excused from our dinner without any sort of bizarre induction rituals that I'd expect from a secret club, but I also knew that members weren't chosen until late fall. So, I guessed that the dinner was simply a taste of the pretentiousness of the club and the meeting of a middle-aged man.

The attendees knew that this meeting was a preliminary scouting event, and so they all went to shake Herman's hand. I didn't bother. What could a glance at eighteen different faces do for an old alumnus' decision? Did he even have any power? The only thought on my mind was to get back to work and earn my place.

I wanted to leave as the room became fraught with bombastic brownnoses. I tapped Micky's shoulder and signaled him to leave, but he waved me off. I sighed and stood there with the rest of the group until the man stopped talking, and people stopped asking questions about his life at Kingsley.

"Young man," he pointed out, putting his large hands on my shoulder as we started to leave, "I noticed you didn't introduce yourself."

He was quite perceptive for noticing, and that's exactly what I told him. "I'm Thomas Walther, sir."

He paused, and his eyes regained some sheen for a moment, "Nice to meet you, Mr. Walther."

I talked with him a little, out of obligation. After only a short time, I turned around and noticed that Micky was nowhere to be seen, and I grew ticked off at him before being dragged back into conversation. "So," he continued, "I believe you've met my stepdaughter."

"I don't know, sir. I didn't realize your daughter went here. What's her name?" I inquired ingenuously. My mouth was dry, having barely drunken any water.

"Elise Poitier," he responded dryly.

My eyes lit up in both shock and fear. "Really," I responded slowly, "She's a good friend of mine."

"I am fully aware of that," he replied with an almost evil undertone, "She speaks of you often during the weekly phone calls I have with her." Out of all my fright was some honest pride. I was glad to have made an impact.

"I'm glad to hear that, sir. I'd like to think that we're good friends," I replied respectfully with a smile.

His face remained unchanged. "I care for my stepdaughter very much, Mr. Walther, having raised her for nearly all my life. Naturally, I want her to do well. Unfortunately, there is no Red Clock Order for women at Kingsley, and so she is without the advantages that I had," he blatantly revealed.

"I understand."

"I'm not sure you do, Mr. Thomas," he snapped, "I want you to stop consuming such large portions of Elise's time."

While trying to remain my calm, I took much offense to his demand, "Mr. Herman, I'm not dating your stepdaughter. I'm just a friend."

"If that's what you consider your relationship, fine, but I want her phone calls to report her assiduous study behavior, not what you and her discussed last weekend while she was supposed to be preparing for a test."

"Respectfully, sir," I said through my teeth, "we were studying diligently on that test, in fact, that's all we've done. I'm not wasting any of your stepdaughter's time, but frankly, I think that you might be with your excessive control over her life." I walked away with steam fuming behind me.

On my way out, a waiter, who was standing next to the door for the entire conversation, stared at me as he smiled with a mocking sympathy. I responded with a stern glance.

Before I could turn around at the door and comment on one more thing, Herman had already left through the exit on the other side of the room. He was speedy for a middle-aged man, I'll give him that.

When I opened the door in a swift but livid motion, I saw Micky leaning against the marble wall next to me. His jacket was placed over his shoulder and his white shirt was creased near his armpits where he placed his crutches. "That took a while," Micky remarked, struggling to return to a vertical balance.

"Yeah," I sighed.

"What'd he have to say to you? Good things, I hope?" I couldn't tell if he meant it or not. Micky often shifted between two sides of carefree playfulness and a subtle, edgy competitiveness. With him, it was difficult to determine what his words implied. At this point, I couldn't trust him, but I'd contain my wariness and pretend to remain kind and cordial.

"Yeah," I shrugged and lied. I decided it would've been best to keep those issues away from Micky. For all I knew, if I had told him, he may have regained interest in Elise and tried to sweep her away.

As we walked down the stairs one step at a time—as a result of Micky's unrefined skill of walking down stairs—the sound of music grew increasingly loud. I recalled that the dance was being held in one of the larger rooms in Commons. Colorful lights and crowded dancers filled the room.

Micky and I exchanged judgmental glances, agreeing how ridiculous the bad music and awkward participants were. Before we could return to the main lobby of the room,

I heard my name being shouted from over the incessant chatter.

Assuming I had either misheard or it was a different Thomas, I kept walking until someone grabbed me by the arm. "Thomas," Elise shouted cheerfully, "were you just going to stop by without a word and leave?"

"Hey, it's Elise!" Micky announced. Elise returned a momentary glance and smile of acknowledgement. It seemed uncomfortable.

"What are you doing here? Shouldn't you be inside already?" I asked while trying to find some way to shield my ears from the overly loud amplifiers. I checked the clock next to the stairs to see that it was already ten o'clock. The meeting had gone on for more than two hours, which was surprising given how dull the entire event was.

"One of my friends has a huge crush on my date, so I made him go with her," she explained without concern. What about you? What are you doing here?"

"I wasn't here for the dance," I reassured.

"You two seem dressed for the part," she pointed at my suit and tie, "last time I checked, a shirt and tie were only required for classes, not evening strolls in the dining hall.

It was a struggle to find a suitable answer, "You know, I just like to dress sharp."

She looked at me, puzzled, for a moment before shrugging it off, "Do you want to dance?"

Micky nudged at me encouragingly and gave me an almost congratulatory wink before he hopped away. "Sure," I stammered.

"We're out of tickets," a middle-aged man yelled to us from behind a table full of cash. From the tweed jacket and maroon plaid shirt, I guessed he was a teacher here with nothing interesting to do on a Friday night except chaperone a crowd of horny teenagers.

"Please Mr. Hart," Elise pleaded, "We just need one extra ticket."

"I'm sorry, Elise," he replied coldly, "we're at capacity and we're only supposed to let in however many tickets we had." Typically, I would've spoken up against this indignation, but I just stood and watched our rejection. I didn't want to go inside. The music seemed unpleasant, and the room's humidity radiated out into the lobby.

She looked down in disappointment as she walked back towards me. From the corner of my eye, I also saw Mr. Herman and Dr. Carter shaking hands and sharing an amicable discussion between old friends. My only thought was to get out of there. "Do you want to go somewhere else?" I asked Elise out of some impulsive thought.

Her hidden disappointment shifted to a warm smile. "Sure," she responded fervently.

I grabbed her hand, which was cold from the non-heated space near the stairs, against my warm hands, which had been heated from the warm, stuffy Bishop Room. The Commons lobby was filled with throngs of people as well, most of them heading out early to break school rules.

Trying to distract Elise from looking over and seeing her stepfather on the other side of the room, I tried to hurry her outside. Before we left, I glanced back to see both Mr. Herman and Dr. Carter glare with burning disdain. Without thought or any consideration, I smirked back at them arrogantly. It felt good.

We took a casual saunter through and around parts of the dark campus, passing by many other pairs of students. Some strollers were couples either sneaking away or just beginning to head to the dance, while others were the ne'er-do-well students who drank and smoked on a regular basis at Kingsley. After twenty or so minutes, we ended up walking back to her dorm, which was located on the other side of campus from my building, as were all the girl's dormitories.

Pairs of students were entering the large, brick building through different windows and doors. One guy looked over at me and gave a wink and nod of mutual congratulations as he escorted his girl into the dorm.

After a few seconds of just standing there, waiting for a break in the waves of people approaching the dorm, I looked at her. Her two-toned dress was scintillating and she looked gentle under the streetlight next to the door.

I wasn't sure of her intentions, but considering the huge inconsistency of that night, I forced myself to go in for a kiss. My heartbeat leveled as she pulled away, smiled softly, and pulled me back to her room. I couldn't place the feeling, but it all felt to unusual, too easy, as if it were undeserved.

We then snuck inside, past the house counselor, who was lost reading "The Bell Jar" by Sylvia Platt and listening to blaring music with the door wide open. Interestingly enough, she was using an antiquated record player to enjoy the melody of Miles Davis in an odd accompaniment to her reading.

When we had reached the lightly painted wooden door, Elise gave me a peck and gently bit her lower lip before she turned around to open the door. I stood there for a few minutes while she looked for her keys. Another kid, being led by a short brunette—who I assumed was the guy's girlfriend or just a loose girl—to her room, gave me a pat on the back as he passed by to the room at the other end of the hall. I smiled in nervousness and excitement until she opened the door and pulled me in by my wrist.

The room was well furnished and decorated appropriately for a girl's dorm. A second, neatly organized bed rested on the right side of the room, which I assumed was her roommate's. Elise reached into her closet and pulled out a sock, which she promptly placed on the door handle. She pulled me in as I felt her, cold from the winter air.

After a few minutes of kissing, I didn't build enough courage to take a risk, and so we only sat there for a while until we were too tired to stay awake, let alone do anything else.

The night ended well, better than well. My stress seemed to be lifted away for the next few hours as I finally slept and dreamt my first dream that I could remember since sophomore year. It was about the Red Clock Order.

CHAPTER 9

I woke up with a jolt. Awake, my thoughts were blurry and incongruent. Behind me was a pale, redheaded girl sleeping in the other bed. Elise had her eyes still gently shut, but my arm was caught under her neck as she lay there on her back.

Unintentionally, I had spent the night, without even signing in at my own dorm. I snuck my arm out from underneath her with little grace. She woke up immediately after with tired eyes and a content smile. Suddenly, I didn't want to leave, but I explained to her how I needed to get back. I felt embarrassed and incompetent for falling asleep so easily, but the late night studying had gotten to me.

Elise understood, and she helped me sneak out through the stairs in the back of the building. The valediction was uncomfortable and uncoordinated. Afterwards, I snuck my way through the quiet, foggy campus of early Saturday morning. Slush and some large mounds of snow covered the path back to my dorm.

My mind was filled with both Elise and the Red Clock Order. The night before, I was drunk with the toxic desire to vindicate myself from the insolence of Carter and Herman. I wasn't worried about being punished with a restricted curfew for missing sign in; now I was afraid that I had jeopardized my only chance at joining the Red Clock Order.

When I reached my own dorm, I tiptoed my way across the hallway. In front of my room's door, I heard the loud snoring of Micky. To be honest, I found the consistent buzzing snore, a sound of steady familiarity that I could depend on every morning, almost relaxing.

Although I knew I'd have to face Dr. Carter at some point, I spent the few hours of the morning awake and studying. My mind, however, kept running adrift, reminiscing about the previous night. When Micky woke up during midday, I developed a strong urge to tell him every detail.

"Tommy boy," he yawned. When he fully came to, he remembered and his eyes lit up, "Tommy boy! How'd it go last night?"

"It was great Micky," I said in my most purposefully blasé voice, "it was really great."

He immediately looked satisfied and secure, as if free from guilt, "My boy's all grown up. So you spent the night?"

"I didn't mean to," I chuckled with a raspy voice and morning breath, "I just held her for a while afterwards, and we both fell asleep."

"Wow, so did you actually fuck her? She seems loose enough," the tone of his voice had become ambiguous, enigmatically unidentifiable.

I was too distracted by my own issues and joys to study Micky's expression. "She's not, and we didn't," I stated defensively and then sighed, "Although I'm worried that I, myself, am fucked because I didn't sign in last night, as if Dr. Carter wasn't already pissed off at me."

"Don't worry, buddy, I signed in for you last night. I didn't know if you'd make it back in time. I guess I was right to do it."

"Thanks man." No longer concerned about Micky, I continued to explain my situation with Elise's stepfather and how he now despised me, and Dr. Carter's hate for me worsened.

"Wow, you've really made some enemies," he commented after I told him everything.

"The worst thing is, I don't know if I'll be able to make it into the Red Clock Order," I confessed.

"What are you talking about?"

"The dinner was obviously for recruiting new members."

"I don't know what you're talking about man. It was just a dinner."

"Oh, yeah, that's bullshit. You know it was for the Red Clock shit."

"Listen, Tommy boy, I don't know what you're talking about. As far as I'm concerned, the Red Clock Order doesn't exist." I was stunned. Micky took this more seriously than I did. For all I cared, such a publicized secret society wasn't really secret if everyone knew about it.

"Whatever, man," I replied.

Seconds later, a loud knock came from the door. It was Dr. Carter, "Ah, Mr. Walther. You're up. A word, please."

I sighed and followed him to his office for the third time that year. On the way out, Micky signaled me to keep quiet. I intended to do exactly that.

"I warned you about Ms. Poitier," he stated as he shut the door behind me. Once again, the orange light gave me a headache. Even though it was morning, he kept the curtains closed, away from the light of a cloudy day.

"Well, you didn't tell me that it was her controlling stepfather who had an objection," I retorted calmly.

Carter removed his glasses and massaged his forehead with his fingers, "David Herman is the senior member and alumnus of the Red Clock. When he has an issue, I have to go through scrupulous effort to deal with it. Now, if you don't comprehend and heed the severity in my voice, then there will be hell to pay for your intransigence, Mr. Walther."

I leaned in closer to his red face, which was hiding in the dark behind the desk. "I haven't the slightest clue what you're talking about," I said slyly, "I don't know anything about this Red Clock Order. If you don't mind, I have a senior term paper to complete."

"I'm the one that chose to invite you to the dinner, Mr. Walther," Carter spoke when I got up from my seat.

"Dr. Carter, I'm not sure what you're—,"

"I chose to invite you over the three hundred other students because of your determination and potential, not because of your grades and definitely not because I like you," he interrupted, "but it was mere chance that I met you. You very well could've been transferred to some other teacher's history course. It was by some grace of God that you caught my attention and are now a solid candidate.

"Now," Carter continued, "Mr. Herman is more subjective with his decisions. Never, though, have I seen such impertinence from a student, let alone from a potential inductee. If you cannot fix your relationship with him, then there is nothing that can be done. You have something to offer the Red Clock, and so you'd better make amends with him."

He caught me dumbstruck. I didn't expect such direct commands, nor did I expect the truth to be what it was. In my room, I found Micky asleep again, this time on my bed. When I saw a pile of drool collecting on the carpet floor above his open mouth, I kicked him softly in the stomach. "You're ruining the carpet, Micky. Get up."

Micky coughed and stumbled back to his room. An hour later, I went to lunch and then the library to focus on preparing finals, which was only two weeks away. When

Kevin Ma

I returned, just before dinner, I saw a torn strip of yellow notebook paper that rested on top of my textbooks on my desk. It listed a phone number and a simple instruction: "call".

For the next ten minutes, I sat there trying to convince myself that Herman was pure evil. The more I thought, the less of a motive for my irritation there appeared to be. "Fuck," I mumbled to myself before going into the hallway to dial.

I assumed that the number was David Herman, because a man with the exact same voice picked up. "Hello?" a low, husky voice picked up the phone.

"Hi, Mr. Herman? Sir, it's Thomas, Thomas Walther," I said. After I introduced myself, I heard the click and a call-ended tone.

But, of course, persistence meant a lot, and so I dialed his number again from my single telephone in the hallway. "Mr. Herman," I addressed in a commanding tone, "I like your stepdaughter, and I don't plan on taking her attention away from her studies. I am just as intent on succeeding in class."

"I'm sure you are," he replied, "but the fact of the matter is that you left with my daughter last night from the Winter Ball, which has existed at Kingsley since before even when I was attending. Don't think I don't know what you did."

"Yes, sir. I know, sir. But—"

"Stop saying 'sir'. It's obnoxious and makes you sound servile," Mr. Herman demanded.

"Fine," I complied, "but you have to understand, I don't mean to jeopardize anything. I only hope that you may find a way to forgive my impertinence."

"I won't hold a grudge against you for it," he said, "so long as you prove yourself as a candidate. If you want any prospect of a respectable life after Kingsley, then you must show your commitment to your own future."

"Yes, sir. Anything." I felt dirty for being so downright submissive.

"Beat your roommate," he said, deadpan. For a second, I thought that he wanted me to literally beat Micky with a bag of pennies, which would've been ridiculous because I would've likely lost the fight.

"I'm sorry, sir?"

"You heard me," he responded, "beat your roommate. It sounds absurd, I'm fully aware, but beyond Kingsley, the world is full of misfortune and corrupt politics. If you ever wish to make yourself larger than a miniscule dot in the world, then you must first make yourself a worthwhile investment.

"Furthermore," he continued, "It's problematic for two roommates to be in the society. Conflicting interests. So, outperform your roommate—sabotage, competition—whatever it takes."

"How do I do that?" I asked.

"If only it were so easy," he replied before abruptly hanging up the phone. I was beyond confused but mostly ticked off.

I was at a loss. I had finally begun to appreciate Micky, and I didn't want to screw him over.

When I returned to the room, Micky was absent, and so I worked in peace and quiet. Sunday morning, I went over to see Headmaster Fitzgerald, who was the only person I could speak to, but the last person I would want to.

"What the hell is so special about the Red Clock?" I asked exasperatingly during a routine meeting, "It doesn't make any sense."

"Well, it's a tradition, Thomas," he replied.

"A tradition of what? A clock with paint all over it?" My frustration was directed more at the Red Clock Order than Micky or Elise. Maybe it was just because I didn't have anything else to blame anymore.

He sighed, "I don't think anybody knows the answer to that."

"Not even the people in the society?"

"No, not even them."

"That doesn't make any sense," I repeated.

"Oh, it makes perfect sense," he assured, "how does anyone know where a tradition begins or why? We can only guess. Whatever the meaning of the clock was, or what the original purpose of the society was, doesn't matter. What matters is what it means now."

"What does it mean now?" I wondered, trying to maintain the same volume of ire over the intrigue.

He glanced at me for a second, "Well that's for you to find out yourself."

I scoffed and exhaled in disappointment, hoping to have heard something spectacular or spine-chillingly exciting. Instantly, all my worries and anxieties came flushing back in.

"Are you alright, Thomas?" Fitzgerald asked, "You seem to have something else on your mind."

I thought for a moment, and told him everything, save for the thing between Elise and me. It's not as if it could've done any harm, so it seemed. At the very least, reciting my issues aloud provided a momentary sensation of relief.

"Wow," he said, "that's quite a situation you've gotten yourself into, Thomas. The Red Clock, though, from the little that I know, has these tests that you must complete, however obscure. I remember a few years back; there was a young man who stood outside in the Kingsley graveyard for three hours during a harsh late winter blizzard solely to prove his loyalty and perseverance. Yours seems more emotional than physical. These tests border on mature hazing rather than perhaps just club loyalty. Still, you have an obligation.

"I'm surprised, though," he continued, "Herman just got upset with you because you wouldn't introduce yourself?"

"Yes," I lied hesitantly.

"He, even when I was in school, was very formal and polite in all encounters," he stated, "Anyways, they are very serious with their secrets. I can't tell you what to do, that's up to you. But if you truly are determined, then you must do whatever it takes. I'm sorry, I wish there was more I could do to help you out."

"But you're the headmaster," I chuckled, hoping that my good relation with him would've provided some benefits.

"That means nothing," he scoffed, "I run the school's educational system, but everything beyond that is out of my control."

"Well, thank you for your time, Dr. Fitzgerald."

"You know," he said, "If my guess means anything, I'm sure that Micky was told to do the same to you."

With a wave, I left his office and adjourned back to my room to review my textbooks and class notes, most of which were sloppy and illegible. Micky walked in and asked me to go to lunch. Commons was quiet on Sunday mornings, yet the food was still plentiful. Muffins, scrambled eggs, pancakes, and various assortments of brunch food were laid out on the first floor. Naturally, Micky stuffed some of each onto his plate until he could barely hold it with one hand.

For most of the lunch, we were silent. I didn't have much to say to him, nor him to me. I couldn't determine whether or not he was thinking of ways to sabotage me or not, until he opened his fat mouth. "We're good buds, right?" he asked as he took a large bite out of a crisp red apple.

"I guess," I responded, caught off guard, "I'd like to think so."

"We've been through a lot. I've punched you; you've kicked me, and so on."

"Sure."

"No matter what though, Tommy boy, we'll still stay friends, right?" he asked earnestly. It felt more like a breakup than a meaningful conversation.

"I don't see why not," I replied as innocently as possible.

"Good," he grinned as he took another bite out of the apple.

This was war. I'm not sure how much Micky knew, but I knew that there would be no courtesies to enjoy. He didn't care, and his unconvincing friendship speech was likely just a tactic to disarm my own worries. I wouldn't let him take me for a chump, yet I was more upset that he had underestimated my own ability.

On the way out of Commons, I spotted Elise. Regardless of my covert attempts, Micky's loud crutches and boisterous actions drew her attention. She waved at me. I didn't know what to do, but I knew avoiding her was best, and so I smiled at her—so slightly that I wasn't sure if she actually noticed—and walked out with Micky.

When he left for his routine afternoon disappearances, I searched through his desk to find any evidence that would detail any faults. This Red Clock was single-handedly tearing me apart, and worst of all, I felt dirty, like some low-class wily scum driven by insane envy.

After a meaningless search, I only found his grandfather's pocket watch, which was worthless to me then. At the moment, I had no real idea of what I was doing or why, except that I felt the need to beat Micky. To relieve some of my grief, I told myself that Micky would do the same, and it was true.

I had abandoned the propriety I'd hoped to maintain at Kingsley, as well as Elise, at the command of a single man. It all counted on the hopes that my obsequious actions would help me get into a good Ivy League college and aid me to a wealthier life. In retrospect, it was all for the pursuit of greed.

Much to my dismay, Micky came back in only a short while. This time, though, he had come back with shoes on both legs. His cast had finally been removed, and he walked around normally. "I feel like a new man," he told me.

His pacing seemed normal and his leg stable, except for some minor swelling. The doctor allowed him to slowly progress into running over the next few days. There were some spots with patches of dead skin, which fell in flaky clumps whenever Micky would scratch it. Jerry and Big Ed came to check him out in amusement of the intriguing but gross phenomenon.

It was a sad and lonely Monday as I sat alone in the back corner of my first period history class. The balance of the classroom was unusual as Elise only glanced over at me a few times while I pretended to listen to Dr. Wright's lecture. The two friends that she often sat with gave me scornful glares on my way out. In exchange, I returned a skeptical look towards them. It wasn't like I had done anything wrong.

"Hey," Elise said as she grabbed my arm after I stepped out of the building, "are you all right?" Her friends were walking right next to her, which only increased the level of my uneasiness.

"Yeah," I smiled dimly, "why wouldn't I be?"

"Well," she said as-a-matter-of-factly, "you've been acting unusual every time I see you. There's something wrong."

"No," I sighed, "I just, don't think we should hang out, or even be around each other."

"Oh, so you're just going to hook up with her and leave?" one of her friends rudely interjected. She was dark-haired and somewhat attractive but was slightly chubby.

Elise gave her friend a harsh glance as I stopped abruptly out of her unexpected comment. "Elise, it's not that," I explained.

"You're starting to freak me out, Tommy, what is it?" she asked.

I looked up at the bell tower, which stood stories high above everyone and rarely served a functional purpose with its hard-to-read clock except for this one occasion, "I have to get to class," I excused.

She grabbed my arm again and held it tight, "What's the big deal? Just tell me now."

"I'm sorry, I can't," I pulled away, "ask your stepfather if you really need to know."

She stood there as I walked away, while her friends consoled her by insulting my characteristics, "He's so stupid," "he's not good enough for you", "look how much of a girl he is, he can't even talk to you." The comments I heard trailing behind me almost made me want to laugh, but it would have seemed out of place to do so.

During squash practice, Elise was absent. "Poitier!" the fat instructor shouted multiple times. It was unlike her to be absent, and I was worried that I'd saddened her too much.

After I had dinner and returned to the dorm, I heard a stumbling noise coming from my room as I approached it. Immediately, I went over to Micky's room in order to assure myself that he wasn't plotting something diabolical. With a recovering leg injury, the school excused him from sports and he had spent most of winter term spending his extra time sleeping.

On the last week, however, he had been acting unusually devious, as was expected from him. "Tommy boy!" he said while rubbing his eyes and pretending to have just woken up.

"What's up, Micky?" I greeted.

"How was squash?"

"Fine," out of my stoic answers, the conversation became both stale and dark-hearted, "have you gone to dinner?"

"No, I, uh," I could see him grasping blindly for excuses, something that I often did as well, "I must've slept through it."

"Sure," I responded sarcastically. I chose not to call his bluff directly, as it would not have ended well, "Well, you better hurry. Commons closes in half an hour."

Hesitantly, Micky stood up. He nodded and smiled before putting on his jacket and trotting off to dinner. It gave me ample time to investigate and recover any stolen belongings of mine. Aside from a few crumpled papers and tossed notebooks, there was nothing out of place.

At night though, I couldn't sleep, feeling that there was a murderer waiting to strike from the next room. This test that we were taking felt like a game organized to amuse a bored puppet master. When I went to bed, I gathered everything I despised about Micky and compiled it up to cook up some hatred towards him. For a moment, I did feel as though he deserved merciless wrath, but the emotions subsided in the morning after some rest.

As the snow began melting away on a sunny Wednesday, varsity baseball tryouts were held inside the gym. Baseball had never been a favorite sport of mine, nor did I even consider it an athletic activity, but I decided to try out with

Micky anyways, who decided that he was ready for varsity conditioning only three days after the cast removal.

"Are you sure?" I asked him.

"For the fifth time, Tommy boy, I'll be fine," he replied, "the physical therapist says that I can run."

"I don't think they assumed sprinting and sliding was a part of it," I noted.

"Pfft. Don't worry about me, watch out for yourself," he said. I smiled to his jovial response.

What I'd hoped to regain was the fondest memory of the sport when I used to toss the ball with my father, back before he earned his multiple promotions to CEO. Often in my kindergarten years, we played in our large, forest backyard filled with blossoming spring flowers and a couple of old cherry and apple trees.

My duration in the tryouts didn't last long, as I was relatively out of shape from only relying on squash as a physical activity in the winter. Without practicing for a year, my throw had become inaccurate and my batting, weak. By Friday afternoon, during the first round of cuts, only the surviving thirty-five made it.

I didn't hear my name, but the lumpy coach, Mr. Jacobs, called Micky's. Head Coach Jacobs was a gym teacher who often smoked secretly on campus next to the gym's trash bins and falsely threatened expulsion to anyone who wanted to report him. Still, his swollen voice and childlike temper provided amusing entertainment, and so no one reported his cigarette addiction.

"It's okay, Tommy boy," Micky comforted after the first cut announcements, "I probably won't make it into the second round anyways." He smiled empathetically, but I could read his self-satisfaction underneath. However, his ankle restricted both his sprinting ability and overall stamina. On Saturday afternoon, after the second and final round of cuts, Micky came to me in disappointment. The look on his face was a rare but satisfying find.

"It's okay, Micky," I comforted sardonically, "now you can goof around in JV. Besides, there's always next year."

"Yeah."

In a vigorous stride to end the term well, I locked myself in a dark corner of the library and just stared at black ink for three hours that afternoon and six hours on Sunday, when I woke up early and waited for the librarian to come open the building doors. My secluded area in the back end of the second floor held a desk with a lamp that flickered from the slightest movement. The heater in the library stacks whirred loudly but was quickly drowned out after ten minutes of focused studying.

By the time I reached the outside again, the sunlight burned my eyes, but it felt good to see moving figures again as opposed to my dead lifeless books. What was really six hours of continuous studying felt like a year of solitary confinement.

When I returned to my room, I heard the familiar question from Micky, "Wow, Tommy boy, where've you been?"

At that point, I had little energy left to deal with this kid. In response, I only made a gargling groan when a kid came knocking at the door. He told me that I had a call on the dormitory phone. On the other end was a heavy raspy breathing. "Thomas Walther?" a man asked.

"Yes. Who is this?"

"It's Coach Jacobs."

What a random call, "Hi, Coach Jacobs. Can I help you?"

"You were on the roster for baseball tryouts, correct?"

"Yes, sir."

"Well we're inviting everyone on the list to fill some spots for preseason practice," he breathed.

"I don't know sir," I looked around sporadically, hoping, for some reason, that there would be an answer, "I'd have to call my parents, first."

"How worthless do you think my time is, son?" he coughed, "It's either yes or no, otherwise I'll keep calling until I find other people."

"Yes, sir. I'll do it sir," I said, my voice shaking.

He paused for a moment, "Good. The practice is in South Carolina and starts on the last Monday of spring vacation. Have your parents send a check of four hundred dollars to the gym office, and come down to pick up a packet with all the details."

"Okay." His wording was brief and straight to the point, which I liked. I didn't, however, appreciate making such a quick choice, considering that I was never a decisive person.

"Remember, stick to it. Many extra preseason kids can get moved up to varsity. Just practice," without a parting word, he hung up. Unsure of exactly what just happened, I called my mother to tell her. She seemed minimally proud, and promised to send the check. The rest of the night was short and sweet with drowsiness creeping up on me in a matter of minutes.

My first exam was scheduled at eight in the morning while almost everyone else had theirs in the late afternoon after a sufficient sleep. Everyone in my English class complained, before my teacher entered the classroom, about how early the final was and how obnoxious writing a timed in-class essay would be.

Evidently, though, my obsessive studying proved well, and I finished my essay, about the imagery of dead children in *Macbeth*, early. My ability to bullshit symbolism had improved. After all, experience was the best teacher.

With confidence in nearly all subjects, I tackled my exams one by one. Finally, it felt good to burn my pencil's lead down to its last inch. On Thursday, the penultimate day of winter term and the last day of finals week, I sat down in the creaking corner chair of Dr. Wright's classroom. Elise arrived afterwards and maintained her concentration in her own space.

History was the only thing left on the list, but it was the course I fretted about the most. The subject itself was so vague and broad, and I had barely paid attention in class during such early hours. "Good luck," the cheerful professor said, almost tauntingly, to us as he distributed thick, stapled paper piles full of questions.

With only ninety minutes, I used up all of my allotted time. To add to more of the calamity, Elise and several others used up all of the time as well. She caught up with me after the dismissal. "What'd you think?" she asked.

"Of what?"

"The exam."

"Hard to say. I barely finished," I responded dryly.

She giggled, I assumed out of courtesy. As I tried to make my escape, she grabbed my arm. It felt unusually calming when she did. "Tommy," she said, "I spoke to my stepdad."

"About what?"

"You know what."

"So you know."

"Yeah," she responded in a soft, smooth voice, "We talked, though. You don't have to worry about him; he just gets a little excessive with his attempts to be a good father.

He wants me to do well, but I basically just told him to lay off."

I smiled at her interesting attempt to relieve my anxiety. I was, however, worried and slightly frustrated about Elise's actions. For all I knew, she may have angered the man even more. Nevertheless, I was glad I could talk to this girl again. "That's a relief," I grinned.

She gave me a long, unexpected kiss. I didn't realize this would be a continuing intimacy. Still, though, I put my hand on her back in an implied agreement. As I opened my eyes, I noticed Dr. Wright passing by with a chuckle. "Have a good break," he wished us.

One of Elise's friends was standing there as well, slightly ticked, with her arms crossed. She cleared her throat loudly, and we both looked over at her. "I have to pack because my flight back home is in a couple of hours" Elise said, "but call me over break."

I nodded as she gave me a peck on the cheek and walked away with her irked friend.

"Why so upbeat?" Micky wondered as I walked into the room whistling and trying to hold back childish laughter.

Out of the combined ecstasy of Elise and spring vacation, I explained everything to Micky in full detail. "Wow," he said, "I thought you just wanted to make out with this girl, but you didn't fuck her, and now you want to date her?"

"Shut the fuck up, Micky," I said, "I'm not really sure."

"Listen, Tommy boy, I don't know what your intentions are, but one girl, in high school? Kingsley has a lot of good-looking girls, and you're in the heyday of your prep school career. There's still a year and a half left of school, and you want to spend it with this chick?"

"You're full of shit," I retorted.

"Maybe," he admitted, "but if your grades start plummeting because she wants you to go grab some food downtown with her instead of you studying like the diligent student you are, then don't come crying to me."

I didn't trust Micky, and I knew his discouragement was an attempt to sabotage me, but his words held truth. My frustration, however, lay with the fact that I was too easy to be persuaded by my tricky roommate's words.

Spring break came in a rush. The snow had cleared and some warmer weather approached the cloudy skies of New England. Convoys of cars of local boarders pulled up next to the main campus as the finals drew to an end. My mother called me to tell me that she was away visiting a friend and that she had sent a driver to pick me up and bring me back to the house. Afterwards, she asked about the performance of my exams before emphasizing the importance of my studies, which only made me feel worse about the circumstances with Elise and me.

With my father on a business trip, I had the entire three-story, seven-bedroom house to myself for the first of the three weeks of spring vacation.

As promised, I called Elise. The first time, we talked so far through the night, that, by the time we hung up, I was eager to call her again just to finish our discussions the previous evening.

Eventually, I reached the painful point where I told her that I only wanted to be friends and fed her hackneyed excuses to distance myself from her and to please Mr. Herman.

"Yeah," she said with a tinge of confusion in her voice, "that's what we've been this entire time. I don't see any reason to change."

"Right, but that's it. We're friends, nothing else," I confirmed.

She paused a moment and chuckled quietly, "Yeah Tommy, that's what we are—just friends." I had no intention of offense, but I felt like I had just yelled and belittled her, which made me feel terrible.

Still, we talked on the phone regularly for the entire week with no end of things to discuss. Throughout the days, I spent a large majority of my time passing a baseball against the wall in the backyard, running in the track at the local gym, and batting at Jordan's—a small facility of batting cages that I didn't know existed until that year—whenever possible.

On Saturday, a few old middle school friends invited me to hang out at one of their houses. While I enjoyed the time alone, I didn't mind some company, so I agreed. Feeling gregarious, I invited my friends, who then called over more people, to my empty house. Before I knew it, I had spent a couple hundred dollars on pizza and hot wings and the house had become a pigsty. Without my consent, a couple students brought over packs of beer.

Calm down, I thought to myself, it's spring break, your house is supposed to be a ruined mess.

The morning arrived and greeted me with a throbbing headache. I only drank two cups of beer and was not at all wasted the night before, but the sunlight was still bothersome.

Cooper jumped onto the couch where I had slept and started skipping around with his canine hilarity. Nancy, our trusted and very lax, old housemaid born in Illinois was picking up spilled cups and said, "Mr. Thomas, your mother would be upset to find out you had alcohol last night."

"I know," I said, scratching my head, "I didn't plan on that. Could you just keep it on the down low?"

"Sure thing, as long as there won't be any more of these occurrences," she smiled politely, "although, you may need to explain to your parents why you randomly spent two hundred dollars."

That was the least of my concerns. "You know my parents, Nancy. My mother loves to spend money but hates to manage it, and my father frets more about his hundred million dollar stock portfolios than anything else," I explained.

She chuckled and began to walk away but turned around after a few steps to speak, "There were three missed calls for you as well while you were away, Mr. Thomas. Before I left, I wrote down a note on a piece of paper, which, apparently, was used as a coaster."

"Really? Who called?" I wondered. It could've been my mother, who would freak out whenever I missed a single call.

"It was a very polite young lady named Elise? She was looking for you. A girlfriend, perhaps?" she inquired curiously.

"No," I chuckled. With each exhale, I could taste the remains of pizza and beer mixed with my typical morning breath, "just a friend, Nancy. I'll call her back, soon." Micky's words rang in my ear. We were just friends, but I still felt that I had a responsibility to call her every day.

Cleaning up the house took the rest of the day for Nancy, with my help. When Nancy was upstairs vacuuming, I decided to give Elise a call.

"I missed you yesterday," she said, "it was your maid, I think, that told me you were with some friends."

"Yeah, I hadn't seen them in a while. Sorry," I replied.

"Are you gonna make it up to me?" she asked teasingly.

I thought about it for a second, "What are you doing next week?"

"I'm going to our house on Martha's Vineyard, why?"

"Perfect. I'll be on Nantucket by Monday. Care to visit?"

"It's a date," she replied. The words resonated in my head. I knew she was being playful, but it put me on edge. What would her stepfather think?

CHAPTER 10

The weekend passed by, and I took the familiar ferry, alone, to the house. Having gone there since childhood, it wasn't at all difficult to make my way to the quaint, yet spacious home. By then, I hadn't gone to the gym or even practiced batting for three days, so my muscles felt weak and my body fatigued.

During noon, I skipped lunch so I could sneak in a quick bike ride on a short path before Elise came. When I came back, I showered and put on a button-down and my Nantucket red shorts. I waited for her down by the dock, and she stepped off the boat with a gentle zephyr blowing through her hair. "Where's your father?" I asked nervously.

"Good to see you," she responded firmly.

I gave her a hug, "Hey."

"He's not here," she explained, "I told him I'd be visiting a friend here. We're good family friends with her parents, so I do have to visit them at some point while I'm here."

"Sure," I nodded. I, for sure, didn't want to be a part of that if the time came.

After settling down back at the house, we went for a leisurely bike ride around parts of the island. My legs were already sore from the bike ride earlier, but it was fun this time. We stopped at a relatively isolated beach and sat watching the waves until the fading sun began to darken the sky. At night, we ate at a casual restaurant on Main

Street, before catching a movie. During the film, I struggled, several times, to keep my eyes open but inevitably failed.

By the time we were finished with the day, there was virtually no energy in either of us, and we promptly went to bed. Through my weary reasoning, I let her stay in the other bed in my room. "I had fun," she smiled as we both rested unmoving on the beds. I still remember that day fondly. I hadn't felt so carefree and without stress since grade school.

It took all of my effort to wake up at noon. "I was already awake," Elise admitted as we gathered items to prepare for the beach, "I just didn't want to wake up before you."

I couldn't help smiling when she walked out with her bikini and shorts. However much I resisted, I couldn't help but notice that she was well-developed, for a lack of a more respectful term.

We went swimming at a private beach that was a ten minute bike from the house. At noon, we just sat in the sand and ate some sandwiches. "I like you," Elise said spontaneously. She had an odd way of approaching things.

"The feelings mutual" I chuckled uncomfortably.

"So why are you so afraid of my stepdad?" she asked.

"I don't think it's relevant," I chuckled nervously.

"It is," she stated, "he's just one man."

"I know," I said. He wasn't, though. He was the man that held my entire future in his hands, and I couldn't even begin to imagine his power.

"So? What?"

"So, nothing," I replied, glancing down at the sand on her chest. I shook off my distraction, "we're just friends. I wouldn't want to upset your stepfather."

"Right," she smiled impishly as she leaned in closer.

Something came over me as I placed my hand on her stomach and moved in closer. I had only exacerbated my increasingly impulsive behavior, but the consequences meant nothing at the moment. After a while, we biked back to the house. When we arrived, it was hard to believe that the whole day had gone by; it had already turned dark, and the dim streetlights were turned on.

Being a naïve teenage boy, I was wildly enthusiastic, and so was she. In the bedroom, I removed the left strap of her bathing suit, and she removed the other in coordination. "Holy shit, I can't believe I'm with this amazing senior girl," was the only coherent thought running through my mind for the rest of the night.

It was only at ten thirty when I noticed that we had inadvertently missed dinner. As a supplement, we finished off a box of stale crackers while watching television. In the morning, I woke up to hear the sound of dishes and chatter downstairs. Looking around, Elise wasn't in the bed or even in the room.

As I walked down and made my way towards the kitchen, I saw my mother, laughing warmly with Elise in a pleasant conversation. "Mother," I addressed. Her presence was very unexpected.

"Good morning, Thomas! You didn't tell me that you'd have a girl over, and a lovely one at that. And for goodness sakes, Thomas, you look like you've been in a train wreck," she pointed at my hair, "go change into some decent clothes." Everything I knew about bullshitting, I had developed from my experienced mother, who would've made a great actor as she never broke her false character. So I couldn't tell if she honestly approved of the unexpected guest or not.

For a few minutes, I thought that I had been dreaming. When I went downstairs to still see my mother there, I knew that I wasn't. "I didn't realize that you were arriving today," I remarked.

"Yes, well, I didn't plan on it," she replied, "but there were some heavy storms predicted and I decided to take an early flight to avoid all that mess. I was hoping to surprise you, but I can see you were already enjoying Nantucket with Elise here."

Elise grabbed my arm good-humoredly. "Yes, these past couple of days have been a lot of fun, Mrs. Walther. Again, I really hope I'm not imposing."

"Not at all, dear," she said in a high-pitched voice, "you said the rest of your family was on the vineyard, am I correct?"

"Yes, ma'am," she replied respectfully.

"Well, if they're not too busy, I would love to have them over for dinner some time, if they don't mind coming over." My heart started pounding. My mother made the worst possible suggestion that I could've hoped for.

Elise, caught off guard, stammered, "I-I'm sure they wouldn't mind." She grabbed my arm tightly now.

"What are you going to do?" I asked, panicking after pulling her aside.

"It's fine, I'll just tell my stepfather the truth," she said.

"That's not funny."

"And I'm not joking. Come on," she tugged on my arm and pleaded, "he's not going to get mad. You'd get a chance to make a better impression. Plus, I'm not sure my lie would've held up well after he calls the people I'm supposed to be staying with."

"Fine," I sighed, and I left the room for her to make her call. Desperately, I was trying to think of ways to reach better terms with Mr. Herman. I thought having varsity baseball on my record might impress him.

"They'd love to come," Elise said as she came back into the kitchen to tell my mother.

"Lovely," my mother replied with a smile.

The next day, Elise and I waited at the airport for his Gulfstream jet to land. He arrived, fully dressed in a business suit, with his wife walking emotionlessly next to him. She stood a good head below him and wore a garish pearl necklace around her neck. Behind them was a ginger-haired kid in bright yellow shorts and a blue polo shirt with the Kingsley seal on it. I recognized him and lost some strength in my legs. It was the same bastard that punched me in the face.

Herman smiled upon seeing Elise and gave her a big embrace before looking over at me. He shook my hand and nodded. "So we meet again, Thomas," he pointed over to the kid, "this is my son. I'm not sure if you know him."

"Harlow Winthorpe Herman, I've seen you around before," he said with a sniveling smile as he reached his hand out.

"It's good to meet you," I said with sarcasm.

"It's nice to meet the boy that's been taking up all of our Elise's time," the mother said in a pretentious accent. It was a family full of conceited members and Elise was at the heart of it as the golden child.

Herman and his entourage insisted on renting a car instead of walking back, so Elise and I left ahead of time. "Why didn't you tell me about your stepbrother, especially the fact that he goes to Kingsley?" I asked, putting the bike in the garage.

"I don't really like to talk about him. He tends to be very aggravating. Besides, it's not important. Why does it matter to you?"

"It doesn't. I just would like to know that you have siblings," I falsified.

"Step-sibling," she corrected.

For the afternoon, I brought them to go sailing on my father's fifty-foot sailboat, which he rarely used given the little time he allocated for leisure. Herman was a natural, and Elise had some experience, but Harlow sat in his ineptness and complained about the leaning of the boat.

While most everyone had gathered below deck, and I was pulling down the main sail, a heavy hand landed on my shoulder. "Need any help?" Mr. Herman asked, setting down his drink nearby.

"Sure," I said, with no other viable response.

As he folded the sail, he mentioned a topic that I had hoped to avoid, "So, you spent a few days alone here."

"Well, I wouldn't say alone. Your daughter was here," I gulped at my bad joke. Clearly this humor was not acceptable, "we didn't do anything, sir, except go to the beach."

"That's hard to believe," he scoffed.

"Mr. Herman, I love your stepdaughter," I lied through my teeth. What the fuck did I just say? For God's sake, I still believed we were only friends. I, for sure, didn't mean it, but my head obviously had no filter for lying. Grinding my teeth, I prayed that Elise, sitting inside, didn't hear me through the open door.

"I would hope so," he said wryly and paused to stare at me. When the sail was covered up, he sighed and picked up his drink again, "You're quite the sailor, just like your father." He seemed to have a change of heart, so I just went with it, being the incompetent fool I was.

"I didn't know you knew my father, sir."

"Well, your father, James Carter, and I all became close friends senior year," he said. I assumed it was because the Red Clock Order applauded camaraderie. He continued, "He was a good man, I expect that you'll prove to be the same." With that remark, he went below deck and left me to motor us in to the mooring.

Dinner at a restaurant downtown was far beyond unnerving. While my mother had little difficulty holding a conversation with the Herman family, every time one of them spoke to me, I felt as if I was saying my last words before taking the electric chair.

Meanwhile, I frantically searched for ways to impress the Herman by telling him about my summer internship and aspiration for baseball. Every time I did this, David Herman would bring up his own son's accomplishments in response: "Harlow is Cum Laude and captain—the only two-year captain, soon to be three-year, in Kingsley history—of the hockey team. He's attending an internship this summer at a private equity firm. Yes, he's going to be a successful young man."

My mother ate up the compliments for Harlow, and I knew the moment we were alone, she would berate me on my insufficiency in comparison to the orange-haired child star.

After the dishes were put away, Herman and his family retired to an inn nearby. When Elise offered, or rather insisted, on staying at my home, David Herman looked displeased but gave me a glance of expectation.

The next morning, after breakfast, Herman, Harlow, and I went kayaking, while Elise, her mother, and my mother sat at the house waiting for our return. Harlow, being the egotistical braggart he was, blazed ahead, paddling at full speed without a clue where to go. David used this opportunity in order to hold a condescending, interrogative discussion with me, once again.

"What line of work do you hope to go into, Thomas?" he asked, drifting along with the current.

"Sorry, sir?"

"An occupation, son, you do know what you want to be, don't you?"

"Well, I always had an affinity for stocks. The ups and downs, the workings of an unpredictable market is exciting."

"You are your father's son," he replied monotonously.

The truth was that I wanted to be nothing like him—away from the family and obsessed with his work—but Herman didn't need to know. "Yes, sir," I replied.

"I have church this Sunday. Why don't you come with us, Elise and company?" He invited. I wasn't sure what he was trying accomplish by doing so.

"I would love to, sir, but baseball preseason begins on Monday, and so I need to return home to pack this weekend," I excused.

Practically ignoring my response completely, he asked, "Are you a man of God?" Was the Red Clock actually a secret society or just some sort of religious cult? Come to think of it, my dad was just as fanatic about his Anglicanism as these two were.

"I'm a man of *a* god, sir," I responded.

"What is it? You don't appear Jewish, and you'd have little reason to be Muslim. Agnostic?"

I nodded and told him exactly what I told Carter.

"I don't believe you don't believe in the Christian God," he said.

"Sir?" I asked, slightly offended.

"So long as we both see eye to eye on monotheism, then we can agree that there's only one God. Your view of Him is what differs, but often we choose bias over comprehension and believe that I see differently from another when, in fact, our two views have more similarity than one might assume," he explained. It was a lot of philosophy to absorb.

"With respect, sir," I countered, "I think anyone who does blindly believe in a god does so because of family tradition or some insecurity."

"Everyone has their insecurities," he responded placidly, "those confident enough to admit it are truly successful."

After some conversation, he began to detail the life he led, more explicitly than at the club dinner. With a mansion in New Canaan and a multimillion-dollar salary, it all sounded spectacular. "People call it luck that brought me all these opportunities," he explained, "but luck doesn't get you into business school, nor does it hand you a promotion. Your place at Kingsley, meeting Dr. Carter, as well as my stepdaughter, which led to my attention to you, was not a series of coincidences. Harlow's life isn't either. My son earned his place in this world, and in return, the world will reward him."

"I understand, sir."

"Make the right choices, Thomas. We'll see how your efforts result, but in the meantime, keep your head up," he encouraged, shifting his heading as we kayaked into the dock, "just don't forget to look around you once in a while to make sure you're not headed in the wrong direction."

As much as I tried to resist, I found his words enlightening. After all, they were insightful words of wisdom.

In the afternoon, Herman and company returned to their plane. Elise gave a tight hug, which was all I was willing to accept in the presence of her stepfather. Before I knew it, preseason training had begun.

Compared to other sports, baseball had a relatively short preseason. While baseball was still a popular pastime, the Kingsley athletic department had cut down its funding, given its depreciating value in the athletics world.

Overall, the training felt like boot camp. The mornings began with a soothing, two mile jog and a protein meal bar followed with batting practice. With a turkey sandwich, heavy on mayonnaise, we would enter the afternoon sweating during a scrimmage. The dinners were just as bad, with fatty pork and a rotten apple served inside a bad mess hall at a dusty, old camp.

The night was free time to ourselves, but few of us had energy remaining. I bunked in a room with six others, half of whom were seniors. They spent maybe ten minutes talking about girls' asses—one of them spoke about Elise, but I just kept quiet—until we all fell asleep from exhaustion.

Micky was absent from this practice, presumably because of his healing ankle, which the Kingsley trainers strongly discouraged overusing.

At the end of the week, Coach Jacobs only privately spoke to one senior player, who was only cut because he was sick during tryouts. On the Friday afternoon, much to Jacobs' dismay, the assistant coach let us jump into the beach, which had been taunting us from our hotel rooms for the entirety of the training program.

While some of the team started picking out girls with good beach bodies to hit on, I, unsure of the protocol with Elise, joined the other half who spent the day playing football on the sand. By Saturday evening, I was back home, exhausted. Sunday came by with a long drive up to Kingsley campus in Windham.

Although the break presented a range of good and bad, I had a hopeful feeling towards junior spring. The trees had regained life early, and the campus was verdant, filled with a spectrum of green.

I caught up with Elise and had dinner at Commons with her, and Micky remained to himself for the initial week. Consistently, Elise and I took turns visiting each other's dormitories.

Fitzgerald invited me to have coffee in the morning, and there was much to tell him. "That's good, that's very good, Thomas," he lauded, "keep it up. One day, you'll look back in your plush leather seat in your fiftieth-story office and wonder how you got there." I laughed, even though that's exactly where I am today.

It seemed that my commitment to baseball had paid off as well. After only two days, the junior varsity coach moved me up, "We can't have you here. The coaches would be pissed to find that we're holding you down here. I spoke with the varsity coaches; be on the main field for practice tomorrow."

"Good job, Tommy boy," Micky awarded with sincerity. His limp seemed to impair his running on uneven grass, and I honestly think he deserved to move up with me, given his effort. However, I felt proud to be singled out.

I didn't seek approval from Carter, although his tense demeanor had uncoiled a bit. In the second week of spring, Carter slipped a small box into my backpack. I didn't realize he did until I found it after returning to my room.

Inside the box was a silver Rolex watch with its face replaced with a red one. Attached to it was a tag that read: "Keep it on."

I hid the watch just before Micky came in. He didn't have the happy face I would've expected. When I guessed that he never received the acceptance, I grew with excitement. Maybe my coincidental connection with Elise and her father had paid off. Even though I had a good sense that that man didn't like me, maybe he had an obligation to accept me. What luck.

It felt good, not the invitation but the feeling of superiority over my roommate. That afternoon, I called Elise, ran over to her dorm and gave her a kiss, for the first time since spring break. "I love your father!" I exclaimed.

"Oh good, that's just what I wanted to hear from you," she joked in mild confusion, "why, exactly, do you have this affection for him?"

Suddenly, I realized the mistake I made. "It's no reason. He just offered me a really big summer internship," I lied.

"Oh, well, I'm glad you're excited," she commented, "I have good news, as well."

"Really? It's a good day, then. What is it?"

"I got into Princeton," she reported.

"Wow, that's really great. But, it shouldn't come as a surprise. I mean, your stepfather went there, didn't he?"

"Well, yeah," her smile waned a little, "but I got in myself. I'd like to think that you'd be more compassionate."

I grinned and gave her a kiss, "I know. And I am. I'm ecstatic for you."

Elise's corpulent, middle-aged house counselor then came out to shoo me away, "It's way past weekday curfew. You're lucky that I won't report you. Now go on, get out." I assumed she wouldn't report me because it would've taken too much energy out of her.

Still, I felt great, like I could lift a car if the opportunity was presented to me.

My performance in baseball practice went well. During the third inning, the coach put me in at second base. The other team, a small Catholic high school twenty minutes from Kingsley, stood little chance against our pitcher, who had a good arm and better aim. Personally I thought I did well, having caught a ball in the air and tagging someone out on a close call.

Elise watched my minimal playing time in the first game, and I went to meet her after the game, but not before I saw her talking and smiling with another kid in the crowd. I managed to suppress my jealousy, however, before the game ended.

Unbeknownst to me for the first few days, we'd begun dating, without even officially deliberating it. I'd found out when one of her friends spoke to me about it. Micky just scoffed when I told him, "Better watch out, then, Tommy boy."

The days flew by quickly. My apprehension grew, as I questioned what would happen. I had worn the red Rolex watch, and kept it close with me but was not sure what to do with it. During lunch, I found Micky and asked him about it at Commons, but he pretended as if he had no idea. "Learn to keep quiet, Tommy boy. People can hear you," he whispered to me afterwards.

Immediately following seventh period, when crowds of people had already left to the gym for practice, Harlow viciously bumped into me with his shoulder. He looked back deviously, and I thought it was unusual, given how I hadn't seen him around campus since the winter of sophomore year. Right after I regained my focus, my watch began beeping loudly. I wasn't sure why, and so I simply turned it off by pressing every single button.

Seconds later, a big, tall guy in front of me approached at a fast pace and placed a heavy, red and gold bag over my head. After some struggling, I stopped moving in order to make the trip less painful. I doubt that I could've squirmed out of the reach of two, two hundred and fifty pound varsity players.

Five minutes later, someone kicked the back of my leg to force me to my knees and then removed the canvas bag from my head. It was rather violent for me, who was hoping that there would be a formal debate and discussion over tea.

The only light source was a thin candle in the hands of a hooded member. Ten other men in dark red, hooded robes stood around me as well. The dim light made it difficult to make out my surroundings, but I assumed it was Galloway House, given what I thought was the same soft carpet at my feet.

Eight other, very confused, familiar faces were kneeled to the right of me. None of them was Micky, and I smiled in the darkness of the room.

"Thomas Walther, you've been tapped," a hooded member read from a thin, hard-covered book next to the candlelight. For a tap, it was rather aggressive and forceful. I don't think I had an option to say no or not.

The voice, which sounded like Dr. Carter, continued, "Your academic and athletic performance have defined your ability. But both are outspoken by your resolve, which indicates the potential success if we are to invest in your determination." I felt used.

Then, another figure pulled up my forearm and tugged off the watch roughly.

From a box, he took out another watch and crudely put it on my wrist. I looked at it, and recognized the Omega Seamaster, a three-thousand dollar watch that my father kept locked in a display case, where he also showed off a picture of him shaking Reagan's hand, in the living room at home. Whenever he stayed at the office late, I would unlock the case using the key he kept at his bedside and blow off the dust of the watch to ensure the conservation of its pristine nature.

The watch had a black leather strap and clean, white face. Nothing seemed unusual except for the bright red hands, just like my father's. For the other members, they underwent the same process, which I spaced out during, with little variation in description. The ritual, however, still sent chills down my back.

"From here on out, your lives take a dramatic turn for the better," the speaker announced after finishing, "but either you take the word of this secret order, which has been in existence for over two centuries, to the grave, or you won't have a secret to keep anymore."

Before being dismissed, we were told to continue wearing the watch. The beeping of the watch's alarm would signal the time for a meeting, which we would be allowed to attend. However, we were also informed that, as recruits, our full part in the society was yet to be official.

I smiled and took in several deep breaths. Four of the other recruits were in my dorm as well, which was no coincidence, and we all made our way silently back to our rooms. The warm spring air felt a little cooler than usual.

Through the struggles and pains of the last two years, everything felt worth it. I felt surprisingly powerful and empowered every time I looked down at the watch. But the previous ceremony gave me the false impression that the rest of Kingsley, and the rest of my life, would be smooth sailing.

CHAPTER 11

Micky, while he never brought up the Red Clock Order, clearly possessed some concerns as to why no recent news had come to him about it. Occasionally, he would become jumpy and nervous. Other times, Micky would grow really irritated and grow frustrated at anything and everything around him. It was strange to see him deviate from his typical behavior, but there was nothing I could say in comfort that wouldn't compromise my own position.

Dr. Carter, while he gave respectful nods of acknowledgment whenever we crossed paths in the hallway, still retained his stoic attitude. On a Saturday afternoon, my watch started chirping right into my ear while I slept.

I looked around and people in the library stared daggers at me as I pressed numerous buttons to try and shut it off. Sweeping all of my books and pencils into my bag, I rushed over to Galloway House. The heated sun against my dark blazer and shirt caused me to perspire rather aggressively.

When I arrived, two of the recruits were about to make their way up. One of them, Jeremy from the club dinner, had the face of an ill man while the other smiled back at me fervently. The latter person was a bright young man by the name of Caleb Letourneau, who proved to be quite boisterous.

"This is pretty awesome," he said to me as we made our way up, "I haven't been this excited since my father took me to a carnival back in Louisiana when I was five." As far as anyone was concerned, his demeanor didn't qualify him as a legacy. He had a subtle twisted accent and smiled almost as much as Micky. If he wasn't talking about "back home," then he was making an esoteric joke, which made him fit the southern archetype perfectly.

The room was resplendent. The carpet floors were a clean, bright red, and two rows of four chairs faced each other on elevated platforms on opposite sides of the room. At the back of the room were two large, unmovable chairs that looked more like thrones.

Above the chair was a red clock, placed in a brightly illuminated space in the wall, with a gold frame and golden laurels underneath it. Finely crafted dark wood walls completed the rich atmosphere of the room. Harlow—who was the only kid, as the son of the senior member, to have ever been in the Red Clock Order for more than a year—sat in one of the two chairs closest to Carter, who looked as if he thought he was the king of the world sitting in his rightful throne.

The recruits were forced to stand in the back, behind the tall wooden chairs. Dr. Carter explained, in formal circumlocution, the responsibilities of the club and its members. He spoke about the financial duties to manage the school's endowment and establishing connections with powerful individuals outside of the school.

The Red Clock Order prided itself on connections. Some notable relations included, or once included, Warren Buffett, Ronald Reagan, the Pope, and a handful of prime ministers.

In addition, Carter mentioned what he called the "Secondary Endowment" which adopted multiple clever nicknames by the members, including "Back Door Cash" and "Student Tax Returns." He reported it as a whopping two hundred and fifty million dollars, gathered over decades by loyal Red Clock trustees, whose names were kept private. The assets were incorporated into the entire endowment, but were untouchable by anyone outside of the society.

Both the club alumni, who received dividends of two thousand a year, and members, who were allowed ten thousand while at Kingsley, could use the funds. The majority of the members often used half the money to invest in something stupid like penny stocks.

Occasionally, alumni would request the use of small portions—of a few million dollars, which wasn't much in the scheme of things—of the funds in order to aid part of a larger investment project, which would almost always provide a considerable return.

It all seemed so surreal, with both the financial obligations and allowances. There was no backing out, though, because once I had stepped into Galloway House for the first time, back in sophomore year, there was no turning back.

Halfway into the hour-long meeting, much to my disgusted shock, Headmaster Fitzgerald entered and sat into the other throne below the glistening Red Clock. He glanced over at me to his left for only a second, expressionless. Shortly after, the meeting adjourned, and my feet had grown sore from standing. Fitzgerald signaled me over, and I walked over in revulsion. I felt betrayed but without an actual knife in my back.

He sat back down in his seat, and motioned for me to sit down in one of the members' seats next to him. In silence, I glared. When I saw he was about to speak, I interceded, "I should've known, but I thought maybe I could've trusted you, above all this crap."

"Thomas, this isn't as much of a serious issue as you may believe," he replied, with composure.

I knew it wasn't. "You could've at least told me."

"That wasn't the point," he argued, "the point is that you developed a powerful interest in this club. With that willpower, you've become the best in your class, and have an incredible future laid out for you, just like your father."

"I don't want to be my father," I yelled with spit visibly flying out of my mouth, "I don't want my future planned out, and I don't want to be a part of this fucking greenback cult!"

It didn't require eyes on the back of my head to see him sitting, motionless, as I stormed out with fury. By the time I had returned to my dorm, my vehemence had subsided, but I still tried to upkeep the same amount of anger as when I left and nearly doomed my own future. As I opened the door to the dorm, I asked myself what the fuck I was doing.

"Hey, speak of the devil. Where've you been, buddy?" Jerry asked, sitting next to Micky in my room.

"I don't want to talk about it," I replied faintly.

Micky had a tinge of a suspicious expression. "Are you okay, Tommy boy?" he asked, "You look like someone died."

"Yeah, fine. Why?"

He shrugged, "No reason. You just look like more of a downer than usual." The insults stung a little more.

To get my mind off of everything, I ignored studying and spent the Sunday with Elise, who was also on a slacking spree after her early acceptance. We spent most of the day downtown, but there wasn't much to say, given that there wasn't much I could tell her.

At night, Carter called me in to his office. I told him that I'd rather not. "Sometimes, the choice isn't yours to make, Mr. Walther," he replied smugly.

I sighed heavily and paced towards the chamber of Hell. He sat down and cleared his throat quietly.

Fitzgerald and Herman were standing in the room as well, and I felt my knees nearly buckle. "'But even if you suffer for what is right, you are blessed," he began, "Do not fear what they fear; do not be frightened. Take courage.' Peter, chapter three, verse fourteen."

I stared down at his desk. "Do you know why I believe in God?" Herman asked.

"No," I replied quietly with a sore throat.

"It's not because I have insecurities. It's not because I'm following my parents, although my father was a Christian as well," he explained, "as a child, whenever I saw a man with his thousand-dollar shoes and imported suit, in comparison with a cheap, penniless vagabond, I couldn't help but ponder the division. To our own comprehension, we explain to ourselves that it's because one man was born with advantages, and he used his own efforts to rise to success.

"In truth, every action we take is planned out from the beginning of time. The opulent Wall Street man earned his riches because his father before him was just as wealthy. Before that, his father was just a poor man who worked his way into wealth as a small Minnesota man in the dog-eat-dog world of finance. But, what started all of this? Something, for all we know, it could be an inconceivable shape, made this happen. We call him God, because He created this for us. Everyone has a plan, Thomas. A nineteenth century politician once said that 'destiny is no matter of chance, but a matter of choice: it's not a thing to be waited for, but a thing to be achieved.' You're a part of this, whether you like it or not, son. The only thing you can do is help make the process go along smoother."

"I don't understand," I spat, "each and every one of you has been feeding me bullshit all year. I've had enough."

"Please, Thomas," Fitzgerald implored, "understand that I've been trying to help you. The Red Clock Order is an invaluable opportunity that you shouldn't turn down."

"No one has ever turned down the Order before," Herman added in a tone that resembled an obstinate, traditional elderly man.

"So why keep me?" I retorted.

Fitzgerald, without an appropriate answer, glanced over at Herman, who looked down at his feet with a frown. Carter responded, "We go through painful processes to figure out who will be chosen. We don't choose twice in a single year, Mr. Walther. The reason for that is because we are never turned down and with good reason."

"You're a good person, Thomas, and I'm sorry. But please, reconsider. I've only been trying to help," Fitzgerald stated contritely.

With that remark, I was dismissed, almost forced, out from the office by Carter.

Somehow, I ended up in my room with bullshit ringing in my ear. I got the feeling that the two, Carter and Herman, thought they, themselves, were gods. Everything he said, though, made sense, but it all felt so flat and disconnected. Micky was asleep by the time I returned, and so I just lay awake in my bed for hours until sleep deprivation got the better of me. Staring at the dark, lifeless ceiling above my bed, I felt lost in my own chaos.

CHAPTER 12

The routines returned to normal for some time. I spoke with Headmaster Fitzgerald during an advisory meeting on Friday, as if nothing happened before that. Although I didn't want to talk to him, it offered a momentary respite from my work and my life.

I went to the next Red Clock meeting and listened as they discussed the financial reports as well as the upkeep of the school. It was serious matters of discussion among high school seniors and facultative teachers, which was different than I had expected. The Red Clock Order just didn't feel special, then, it felt like a job.

"There are a lot of financial duties," I confessed to Fitzgerald, still inside Galloway House after the meeting, "I didn't realize this club would be so oriented towards economics."

"That's what capitalism was founded on, invisible money," he joked as he smiled charmingly with his legs crossed, "success is measured in wealth. That's why the richest and most 'successful' people all work with hedge funds or stocks, and that's what the Red Clock believes in. Now, I was never in the Order, I was just asked to perform administrative duties. Dr. Carter, however, was, as one of the few exceptions, a member that didn't turn out to be some hedge fund manager. He chose history as his major with some philosophical studies on the side.

"From the few friendly conversations I've had with him, I've learned that he travelled the world studying books before settling down as a teacher here with his family. Even at Kingsley, I remember he would spend much time reading books about the spread of the Muslim empire or the Crusades. Yes, it was his passion, but never his dream."

"What do you mean?" I flinched every time he brought up Carter or the Order, but it was something I had to struggle through.

"He always wanted to make money and settle down with a bucket of cash and millions stored in the bank, I mean, who didn't? It was painful that he had to pursue history. He never wanted to be such an enthusiast, but he was. It's odd how the brain can create such contradictions."

He stood up and put his hand on my shoulder, "I'm glad we can be friends, Thomas." I nodded, and he shook my hand. "Feel free to stay as long as you want," he handed me the keys, trusting that I would lock up, "I just wouldn't touch anything, if I were you."

Sitting there, with barely even a thought, I stared down at the red carpet. When I checked my clock, it read half past ten. I stood up to leave, but the Red Clock got my attention. Upon closer examination, the clock's glass cover was crudely painted over with a dark, red tint. The frame had chips in it but still maintained its color which made me believe that they were crafted from real gold, at a fairly pure quality as well.

At the bottom of the frame were some small font words. It was difficult to read, but stepping on Carter's chair, I saw that it was a quote, finished off with "Peter 3:14," the same quote that Carter fed me no more than a few days ago. It all seemed so mysterious but unusual.

When I returned to the dorm, Jerry was there again. "Hey, it's Tommy boy," Micky acknowledged cheerfully.

"What's going on," I asked dryly.

Jerry looked at Micky, who gave him a shrug, and then glanced around the room covertly. He shut the door all the way and locked it. We then went inside to Micky's room and closed his door. "What the hell is going on?" I demanded.

Jerry then took out a plastic bag, and inside it were thin, rolled up pieces of paper that were shaped like cigarettes. "Is that . . ." I started.

"Yeah," Micky smirked mischievously.

"What the hell are you doing with weed, Jerry?" I asked, "Where'd you get it?" Both of them shushed me.

"Keep it quiet, loudmouth, you don't want Carter or Gerald finding out about this shit. The school's already pissed off about this stuff as it is. Half the campus smokes, bud, it's not hard to find a student who sells," Jerry replied. He placed the plastic bag back inside his coat pocket.

"How long have you had this?"

Jerry gave me a pat on the arm and smirked conceitedly, "We've been smoking since freshman year, faggot."

"Why didn't you tell me?" I whispered angrily.

"It's not a big deal. We didn't think you want to join, but the cat's out of the bag. It's not a big fucking deal," Micky replied eagerly and impatiently, "So, Tommy boy. Are you in?"

"You're gonna smoke it right now?"

"No, dipshit, we're going outside," he replied.

"I don't know about this," I looked over at Micky, who was agreeing fully with Jerry. I knew he was eccentric and often spacey, but I thought he'd have at least some sense of responsibility. "This shit will kill you."

"No. Actual smoking cigs will kill you. This will just calm you and pass the time," Jerry said. He looked over at Micky, "Forget it. I told you, Micky, Tommy's too much of a tard to want to do this."

Micky looked over with an encouraging face, "Come on, Tommy boy. It's not hard to tell that you're stressed out as fuck. Just come and smoke with us, it's just one time."

"Yeah," Jerry said in a mocking voice, "don't be prude, *Tommy boy*."

"Come on," Micky said as he pushed me out the door. It felt good to be outside in the cooler air, but I still had my doubts about it. I thought about what I'd say to convince them otherwise when they pulled the joints out.

"Here? This isn't the usual spot," Jerry asked skeptically when Micky stopped. It was just outside main campus, right before the woods started, a few hundred feet behind a girl's dorm, Elise's dorm.

"Yeah, Micky, I don't think this is a good place," I said, nervously.

"It's fine," Micky replied, "No one ever comes back here. A bunch of people smoke here, too."

"Fuck it," Jerry said, taking out his plastic bag, "I don't care if I get caught. I hate this fucking cutthroat school, anyways."

"Dude, this is Elise's dorm," I pointed and whispered to my roommate.

He gave me a falsely assuring pat on the back, "It's fine, buddy. This is a prime smoking spot."

After spending five minutes struggling to get his lighter started, Jerry finally lit it up and took a long drag. When Micky handed it to me, I was hesitant to take it. "Well, you're already here, Tommy boy. If you get caught, you might as well get caught high."

It was true, there wasn't much worse I could do. So I pushed myself past the wall of reluctance, and took short, weak inhales.

Jerry and Micky laughed at my prudish behavior. It was clear I was a novice. The smoke had a stale, oaky taste that was harsher on the throat with each progressive inhale.

"Hold it in for a few seconds," Micky advised.

It took a while, but the smoke slowly began to feel more familiar. Eventually, they decided to smoke a second joint, and I didn't complain. Besides the thorn pricking my arm, I felt much more relaxed. The second one felt smoother, and thoughts of the Red Clock Order and other stress seemed completely trivial, until we were caught.

"Fuck!" Jerry said, as he saw a bright flashlight in the distance approaching us.

Jerry quickly put out the joint and stuffed the plastic bag into his pocket. There was nowhere to run without getting caught, the branches and bushes had us trapped. Micky jumped up and looked around. As the figure approached us, I could make out a large round figure and the sound of a tiny dog on a leash barking effeminately.

"What are you doing?" said the voice of Elise's house counselor, a voice I had become familiar with after staying past curfew multiple times. She was likely just walking her dog, but the cigarette light and loud rustling probably got her attention. She sniffed the air a couple of times, "Is that marijuana?"

"No, ma'am," Micky responded, with his hands in his pockets, clumsily trying to keep his cool.

Demandingly, in her husky voice, she commanded us to wait inside the common room and wait until our house counselors were contacted. Micky kept staring at his hand and would wink and speak to a few girls that passed by. Meanwhile, Jerry laughed at nearly everything. Both their eyes were glassy and the whites were noticeably red.

As chance would have it, Elise came down to the common room. I sighed and tried to hide myself by sinking lower into my seat.

"Micky? Thomas?" Elise looked over at the both of us.

"What's up?" Micky greeted as he kept his focus on a single floor tile.

"What are you doing here?" she wondered.

"We," Micky replied nonchalantly, "Or Tommy boy, rather, wanted to see you. We couldn't let him go by himself so late at night."

"Really? Why didn't you just call?" she asked me.

Not a single plausible answer came to mind. The rotund house counselor saved me by telling her to keep away from us. She shook her head at me in disappointment and chided me. "I knew you were bad news. Stay away from Elise."

"I called your house counselor," she continued, "go back to your dorm, he'll be waiting."

"How about we light one last one up before going down?" Jerry offered as we neared the dorm, "I bet his harangue would be twice as fun, then."

"Fuck you," I attacked with deep concern.

"Fuck you, too," he responded cheerfully. Micky remained silent on the walk back.

We slowly entered the dorm, and Carter stood there with his arms folded in an intimidating manner. He escorted us to his office, and we sat there, still feeling the effects of the plant. Jerry relinquished his plastic bag and remaining three joints while sitting there in a daze.

In a composed, respectful tone, he told us that there would be a punishment involved, likely in front of a disciplinary committee. He requested me to stay after excusing the other two. Micky patted my shoulder and gave me a supportive nod.

"Dr. Carter, I didn't mean to do it. It was just an impulsive idea, and I wouldn't ever do it again," I whined.

"Of course, you meant it," Carter said amidst my wailing, "and I'm sure you would do it again. You're part of a brotherhood, Mr. Walther, one that runs and funds this entire school."

I sighed, and a wave of pressure exerted from my lungs, "But how?"

"A disciplinary committee slip has to be signed and filed by Administrator Hastings."

"Is he part of the society?" I asked, expecting to finally know the man behind the signature.

Carter's neutral countenance turned into a slight smile, "I am the administrator. The society is the administrator. Everything goes through the club, ipso facto, through me." I sighed.

"And Micky?" I inquired, returning to the subject.

"Those two, I cannot help," he said abruptly.

"But they're my friends."

"There cannot be exceptions for every Kingsley student, otherwise parents would complain, and this school would earn a bad reputation," he said, "you would also be wise to keep your friends distant. In the real world, your friends could turn on you in an instant."

"Respectfully, Dr. Carter, this isn't some sort of political business world," I retorted, "this is Kingsley." Those two terms, however, later proved to be synonymous.

I returned to the room and stared down at my desk. "What'd he say to you?" Micky asked from his room.

"What?" I didn't know what to say to him and would've much preferred to have just gone through the rest of the weekend in silence.

He walked into my room, "What'd Coach Carter say to you?"

"Nothing," I shrugged, "he just told me to be careful."

"That's unusual," he remarked.

"Why would that be unusual?"

"I could've sworn that guy had some sort of hatred towards you. You said it yourself."

"I know," I sighed. Confidentiality had always been a weak facet of mine, and holding such a big secret just made it all the more of an agonizing effort.

Sunday morning, when I had woken up well before Micky, as typical on a weekend, Dr. Carter entered my room and handed me two thin pieces of paper. He whispered, "I trust you'll know what to do with it, but either way, it must be turned in to the Dean of Students."

The slips detailed the request of disciplinary committee meetings for Micky and Jerry, with the familiar signature of the acclaimed Administrator Hastings. It felt like an awful lot of power, deciding my best friend's fate.

Kingsley, like most boarding schools, took marijuana possession and use far too seriously for something so common. I knew that the committee would certainly decide on expulsion.

Micky had his downsides, but we were still friends and roommates. If he was anything like me—sad, stressed, and hiding behind a deceitful guise of gregariousness—then he deserved a second chance. As he snored loudly in the other room, I tore the slip up. Jerry, on the other hand, was a douchebag, and so I turned his slip in without hesitation of any kind.

I sighed and hoped that I had made the proper choice, for him and for myself. At the very least, I was still on the side of safety, protected by the Red Clock Order. Nothing made sense anymore, though. But then again, nothing ever did.

A week later, the other members and I were given the opportunity to participate in the very tedious discussion of managing the endowment. Afterwards, Fitzgerald asked me, in what I considered a very uncomfortable conversation, about my grades and classes. "Fine," I responded, deadpan.

I returned to the dorm to find Micky in a particularly exaggerated sulking mood. "How's it going, Micky?" I asked him, ignoring his brooding.

"Not much, Tommy boy," he said. He looked focused, serious, and intent on accomplishing some goal. None of those traits seemed to ever be a part of his wide array of temperaments.

Without much thought, I returned to my desk and took out my notebook to continue working on an English paper. Writing persistently with a pencil was, by far, the easiest way to develop a sore hand.

"Hey Tommy," Micky came over to my room and sat down on my bed while putting on my mitt and playing baseball. He had returned to his normal behaviors and I thought nothing of it.

"What's up?"

"How's varsity?"

"It's not much different, I guess, except that people tend to make a bigger deal about winning games," I shrugged, keeping my concentration towards the paper, but finding difficulty in thinking of what to write. It was peculiar; Micky almost never talked just for banter. Often, he talked only to figure something out.

"Look, Micky," I continued, "is there something you need? I just need to finish my essay right now."

"Fine," he got up and left to the dorm hallway, "just let me know when you're done."

He didn't return for a couple of hours, and I didn't finish until he was fast asleep. I wanted to dissect his odd manner, but the club meetings had already made an out-of-place intrusion to my obstinate schedule.

After he woke up, we both went to lunch together. "So did you get the slip?" he asked as he stockpiled slices of French toast.

"What?" I asked in response, slightly concerned.

"The note thing, about the DC meeting. My meeting's in a week, and it's in the morning, too," he said, still indifferent.

Instead of lying, I made a soft grunting noise to satisfy his question. I spent the next few seconds wondering if I had only dreamed ripping Micky's slip up. How else could that have happened?

"When's your meeting at?"

"I don't know," I said. Sooner or later, though, I'd have to tell him the truth.

Micky then explained how he spent the better half of his night talking to Mr. Gerald and Dr. Carter about his options. Apparently, the punishment was always severe, and there was no way to leave the meeting with at least a blemish on his record. With a group of peers judging his fate, it all seemed pretty intimidating, as if the idea of it was something constructed from nightmares.

"Jesus, man," I consoled, "I'm sorry."

"Don't feel bad for me yet," he responded, "You got DC'ed too, remember?"

I didn't speak.

When I returned to the dorm, I knocked on Dr. Carter's door. Not hearing a sound on the other side, I decided to take a few books and wait for him outside. "Mr. Walther," I heard indistinctly after I had fallen asleep on the chair in the hallway, "Is there something I can help you with?"

His wife and young twin daughters came in behind him, all dressed in modest formal attire for what I could only assume was church. Carter kindly told his wife to go back to the house as he invited me into his office.

"Could you explain to me something?" I asked him in a strict tone. It appeared that Carter's emotionless stare had lost its intimidation, and I had grown more confidence, which almost bordered on snobbishness, in my own ability.

He gestured for me to speak, "You have my attention, Mr. Walther."

I sighed, "I tore the slip up."

"Really," he remarked apathetically, "I expected as much. I was hoping, though, that you'd learn on your own and do what's right."

"What do you mean?" I demanded, growing increasingly angrier.

"Shouldn't it be obvious?" he said as he placed some books back into his shelves, "Mr. Walther, Micky would just as well turn you in if he knew that he was safe and his academic rival would be gone, freeing himself up for Harvard or Princeton with one less competitor."

"What?" I said, thinking he just fed me the biggest pile of hogwash I had ever heard. "If you were just going to turn the slip in anyways, then why didn't you just tell me?"

"I didn't file the request for the meeting," he said haughtily, "It was Administrator Hastings."

Just when I believed that Carter was a decent, almost wise teacher and Red Clock alumnus, he managed to find ways to piss me off more. With a man as condescending and self-righteous as Dr. Carter, there was no getting around it. Having learned my lesson, I stomped out the room indignantly, slamming the door behind me.

Although Carter managed to severely upset me for the thousandth time, I couldn't do anything. From experience, I learned that either my own consciousness would disagree with my anger, or confronting the malicious house counselor again would distress me more. So I left it alone, and I woke up fine, with only a small burn leftover from Carter.

Chapter 13

By the second half of spring term, I'd realized that there would only be four weeks left before Elise would be gone. To make the best of it, I spent as much time as possible with her, but trying to forget about everyone else when I was with her proved to be difficult. I also got the feeling that Elise had other things on her mind as well. Nevertheless, I was glad to be with her.

Micky, as well, seemed to speak to me less with each passing day and started to lose his patina of exuberance. The dorm registration forms next year were handed out, but neither of us discussed the plans for our senior year. Instead, I applied for proctor at the current dorm, not wanting to leave the convenience of Dr. Carter's power over the rest of the school, however appealing the idea of a possibly non-threatening house counselor was.

At the previous club meeting, Herman came down to campus again to personally hand us recruits our club jackets, which were personally tailored for each person. The expensive, silky feel of some sort of linen blend of the jacket with its clean-cut embroidered patch of the Red Clock only reminded me of how much of a bitch it was to deal with the complications of the secret society.

Still, as we all walked out with our jackets, Herman and members included, I couldn't help but feel superior and potent. Instead of withholding our secrecy that night and hanging up our coats, I laughed and joked with the four other members from my dorm as we walked the dark paths in campus. Girls smiled at us and guys stared in discreet envy as we headed back to the dorm in the dark.

When I had returned to my room, Micky was just about to walk out. In consistency with his regular hours, I'd assumed that he probably would be out of the dorm or asleep by the time I returned. Yet, for some reason, a part of me had hoped that he would find out. He looked at my jacket and sighed.

"Look, Micky," I said as he set down his backpack.

"It's alright, Tommy boy," he said as he chuckled, "I'm not mad. I get it." I was worried that he might abruptly burst into a hysteric rage.

Promptly, I took off my jacket and hung it up inside my closet. I sat down in my desk, and he stared down at the carpet without a word. Afraid to disturb the tranquility, I returned to my work while occasionally looking over at Micky, who was fiddling with his pocket watch.

"I know you're supposed to keep quiet, but you should've at least told me, right?" he said abruptly, mildly smiling.

"You know I couldn't have, Micky," I said, unsure of what to say.

"Right," he nodded.

"You didn't get in trouble for the weed, did you?" he asked quietly.

"Well," I chuckled softly, "I wouldn't say I didn't get in any trouble. I mean, Carter got pretty pissed off with me."

He nodded again, "But you didn't get into as much trouble as I did." He paused, "I don't even know if those bastard teachers and kiss ass students will let me off easy."

I made a weird coughing noise and thought it inappropriate to do anything else.

He stared at the carpet and laughed, "Hey, I guess we're even now."

I shook my head in confusion.

"I mean, I fuck Elise, now you're fucking her, and now I'm fucking fucked."

"What?" I heard what he said but I didn't want to believe it because it just didn't make any sense.

Micky looked up. "Oh, so you really didn't know. I nailed that girl first, Tommy boy. Nailed her sophomore year. Jesus, you'd think after all that studying, you'd be smart enough to realize that I hooked up with Elise, not that fucking freshman," he remarked, "and then I screwed her again when you were dating her." That second part, I assumed was an impulsive lie out of spite. It was impossible.

"You're a lying bastard," I yelled at him, "that's a load of crap."

"It's not, Tommy boy," he shook his head conceitedly, "You wanted to know why I let you have her. Now you know. I told you I'd get her first. But it's all good and fair now, because we're even." He repositioned himself on my bed.

In a blinding flash, I ended up with an oncoming pain in my knuckles and Micky, shaking his head in recovery, was laid back on my bed. Some drops of blood were on my bed sheets.

"Shit," Micky grunted as he rubbed his face. Immediately, he jumped up from his bed and tackled me to the carpet ground. Repeatedly, he attempted to kick me with his leg, which was still frail and thin in the process of recovery.

Standing up, I was hyperventilating. Micky glared at me, while still keeping a smile, and stumbled back into his room. In spite of the millions of thoughts racing through my mind, only one crossed mine, to find and confront Elise.

Curfew didn't matter to me in my frenzied rage, thinking that I was practically untouchable with the Red Clock Order behind my back. With a headache, I ran to her dorm. Upon arrival, I knocked on her window on the first floor and she opened up, confused. "Hey. What are you doing here? You could've at least called," she questioned with a smile, "it's way past curfew, and for some reason, my house counselor still hates you, you know."

"Can I come inside?" I asked brusquely.

"I guess," she said, looking around inside her room, "but hurry."

Gracelessly, I removed the screen and crawled through the window. The metal edge of the frame scraped against my stomach, but the minor soreness was the least of my trepidations.

"I know it's a Saturday, but I'm really busy," she informed me, "I have a ten-page paper to write, which I haven't even started yet. I don't really have time for anything, Tommy."

I waved off her statement as I still maintained my heavy breathing, "Did you cheat on me with Micky?" I had to know.

"What?" she recoiled, taking offense, "no, I didn't. Of course not!"

"Well, what about before. Last year? Don't lie to me," my legs were begging for rest, but I just couldn't sit down.

"Tommy, are you all right?" she asked. I knew she was feeding me distractions, and I just didn't want to go through it.

"Answer the fucking question," I had never sworn at her before, or at any girl for that matter, but the thought of Micky and his devilish smile just enraged me.

She stuttered, and then sighed in surrender. "Tommy, I'm sorry."

"I don't want to hear it," I continued to step around the room frantically, "I just have to know. Why didn't you tell me?"

"It wasn't important, at least I didn't think so," she put her hand on my arm and tried to slow my pacing.

"Of course, it's important. Would you even want to be with me if you didn't screw Micky first?" My voice was rising in fury. I wasn't sure if what I said made sense, but it didn't matter at the time, "do you even give a shit?"

"Yes, I would, and I do," she assured, "Tommy, of course I do." Her voice had become higher-pitched, sounding smooth and breathy. She started to cry, but I just couldn't stay in the room.

"Forget it," I had only gone to see Elise in order to hear it from her. Upset, I left the room through the door and went down the hallway. The house counselor had her dorm room closed, and so I left without an issue.

A few lamps lit my path, but it may as well have been pitch black, because I didn't know where I was meandering off to. For a couple of hours, I sat lugubriously on a cold stone bench near the main campus.

Above the croaking frogs and bothersome mosquitoes, my ears were ringing and the back of my head felt sour. Honestly, I wasn't sure if my anger was towards Elise or Micky. When my ire diminished, it seemed wrong for me to have so scurrilously attacked her.

I sighed. When my clock read around one in the morning, I headed back to my dorm room. There was nothing even close to appealing about waking up the next morning. So I slept through noon. For the first few minutes after I woke up, I thought about everything that had gone wrong. Elise, Micky, Carter . . . who wasn't a fucked up asshole ruining my life?

A couple of weeks passed by, and there was no friend to talk to. Micky returned to normal and spoke to me with his smiley exterior, but I just didn't want to talk to him, and he knew it. Seeing my roommate just brought more hate towards both him and me. Elise would show up in history and provide only cold glances while remaining dejected. It was heartwretching, to say the least. My chest hurt just thinking about it all.

I had only Fitzgerald to talk to, who I would continue to meet with on a weekly basis. My recent grades had weakened in the past couple of weeks by only a few points, but the depreciation was dramatic to me. However, I would always feel embarrassed about reporting any indication of a poor performance, and so I kept my grades only to myself. With all my complications, much of my life was withheld from Fitzgerald.

"Are you doing all right, Thomas?" he asked sincerely, "you seem to be a little, I don't know, off, recently."

"Yeah, I'm fine," I replied, "it's probably just a sleep deficiency."

"Well, that seems to have been going around a lot for the past eighty years or so, after college began to actually become significant," he joked, "just make sure that you get enough sleep. Growing tall is important. You can always complete your work in the morning before classes."

"You're right, thanks," I acknowledged. It seemed uncomfortably weird for him to tell me to watch over my growth, but he had been giving such advice quite frequently, lately.

During lunch period, I found Elise sitting at a small table with a few of her friends. "Elise," I sat down in the empty seat next to her, "can I talk to you?" One of her friends scoffed.

"What?" she kept her focus at the salad in front of her, "there's nothing to talk about."

"Can we just talk in private?" I urged.

She sighed and looked at the clock above the doorway, "I have to go get ready for class, Tommy." She picked up her plate and left with her table of friends. I sat there, alone, thoughtless.

What had happened to me? I pondered as I walked out of the dining hall. By the time baseball practice began, I kept suffering pulses of disappointment whenever the thought of any part of my life came into my mind.

A few minutes before the next meeting, I felt a sudden rush of repugnance upon seeing the Red Clock jacket. Its smooth and expensive material sickened me, and the blazer felt tight, restricting, and uncomfortable. It was depressing, not knowing where to go from there. Everyone was oblivious to my own problems, and hiding pain—hiding weakness—was the most difficult thing to do.

"Dr. Fitzgerald," I approached him after the conclusion of one of the advising meetings and everyone had left the room, "can I talk to you for a second?"

"Well, of course you can Tommy," he returned to his chair, "And you can call me George. I'm sure we've been through enough conversations between friends to cut the formalities. So what can I do you for?"

"Dr. Fitzgerald," I addressed, refusing to accept his gratitude, "this may seem a little odd, but I need some advice."

His smile changed into a concerned expression, "Sure. What's wrong?"

"Nothing's wrong," I lied. There was nothing that I actually wanted to tell him, but I needed to say something, "I don't know what I want to do in the future."

He looked confused, "As in, you don't know what line of work you want to go into?"

"Or anything else, for that matter," I continued, "What college major, what company, I mean, what am I going to do for the rest of my life? Everyone else seems to know, but I . . . I seem to be floating adrift in an endless ocean."

My mindless complaint wasn't getting through to him either. What I said barely made sense, yet I was hoping that in an instant, he would understand all my problems without me having to explain them. "Thomas," he said, "The Red Clock has connections to a number of different sorts of companies with exclusive, competitive internships. Why don't I sign you up for a couple this summer, and you can try them out?"

I scratched my head and sighed, "No. Thank you, though, Dr. Fitzgerald. I'll be all right."

My progress was dim. The warm spring air only added to the agony, given how limited my time outdoors was. Seniors played touch football on the lawn, and my legs were aching for physical activity of some sort.

Baseball had me moving very little, given that I rarely ran around except for the sprints at the end of practices that I could barely keep up with. My day went by with eating, sleeping, studying, and the occasional conversation with the Headmaster.

With nothing left to do, no one to talk to, I sat in my room or in the library studying. It was Headmaster Fitzgerald who was the only one that seemed to give a shit, like the father I never had.

Then, the last piece of my world crumbled. "Sit down," he said on a Friday near the end of spring term, "there's something that I would like to speak to you, about, Thomas."

"Sure," I smiled politely, "What is it you wanted to discuss?"

He sighed, and I already knew that it was something unpleasant. Having dealt with a multitude of bad news in the past couple of years, I just didn't want to hear it. "Dr. Fitzgerald, if I may," I interrupted before he got the first word out, "if it's something that would disappoint me, I'd rather not hear it. If it has something to do with my academics or if it's even something as ridiculous as I have to get beaten with a sock of pennies for club initiations, God forbid, then I just don't want to hear it."

The frail headmaster looked surprised, but not stunned. "It's none of that, but that's quite an imagination," he remarked jokingly, "it's actually something much different."

I looked up and nodded for him to proceed. For the couple seconds of silence, I tried to think of every possible piece of disappointing news that he could give.

"No matter what I tell you, remember that no one is to blame," he said. I nodded. "Your mother wanted to be here for this, but she's out travelling," he sighed. Now I was confused, and this had me severely worried. For a split second, I knew what he was about to say. "Your mother and father have been separated for some time, and their divorce was recently finalized. I'm sure they wish they could've told you this themselves."

"What?" I chuckled nervously as I sat up from the chair. It was uncomfortable to hear, but not at all shocking. Since before my birth, my parents had never communicated well, constantly bickering in the other room, thinking that I couldn't hear them argue. This information seemed ill-timed. My throat felt tight, "I didn't expect my parents to tell me this, but why'd they choose you as an advocate?"

"Well," he fiddled with his watch, "that's the other part."

"Oh, great," I murmured under my breath. I had begun sweating, and the room felt extremely warm.

"Your mother and I," he paused again; hearing that phrase, though, was peculiar and unfamiliar, "are moving in together."

"What the fuck?" I exclaimed. I had never had interest in my mother's affairs, but this was just preposterous. What came to question, then, was if my mother had cheated. It doesn't matter if my parents had grown apart; it's still considered adultery. "So my mother cheated on my father with you?" I wanted to punch the table, knowing full well that I'd probably sprain something.

"You have to understand," he explained, "Your parents were growing apart, and I had nothing to do with your parents' divorce."

"You don't have to explain anything; I already understand. You're a fucking asshole, and you're lucky I'm not kicking your ass right now," I exclaimed, disregarding the students passing by outside who could probably hear muffled yelling.

"Thomas," he said in a soft, yet strict tone.

"No, you know what? Fuck you!" I shouted before slamming his office door behind me. A couple of students, who had probably heard me, near the office looked at me and stifled uncomfortable laughs.

I couldn't trust anyone, anymore. While I had always been a recluse, mentally, I was now physically and completely alone. The last person I could talk to turned out to be a part of a sinful affair with my mother.

The universe did deserve some congratulations, though. The news was well timed in a series of ill-fated proceedings, all of which deteriorated any value left in my life.

I thought and thought; first about how furious I was at Fitzgerald, and then about how nothing in my life was real. My part in the Red Clock Order wasn't even because of my own effort. It made sense; I couldn't have had an advantage just because I was a fourth generation Kingsley student because that meant nothing. My induction test was too easy, and Herman and Carter didn't have any reason to have shown the slightest interest in me in the first place. Carter was right; everything had been planned out for me, not by God, but by a single, frail, mild-mannered Headmaster.

As I returned to my dorm, a hot, fiery rage built up inside of me, and I felt dizzy. Although the Fitzgerald matter was the latest thing to have ticked me off, I couldn't help but think about Micky and Elise as well. "What's up, Tommy boy?" Micky greeted as I walked in.

"Fuck you," I muttered. My breathing was heavy and shallow, and I took my blazer off from sweat. Sitting down on my bed, I felt an incredible pain in my chest that I hadn't noticed before. Seconds later, I was on the ground, writhing.

For what felt like the next hour, I faded in and out, as if it were a dream.

I woke up with a bright light breaking through the crack of my eye slits. The room I was in had spotted white tiles and milky green wallpaper. My right arm felt tender as a tube was stuck into my forearm, and a clear liquid was running through it.

A woman, a nurse, looked over at me and smiled, "You're awake." She looked in her mid-thirties and carried a clipboard around, scribbling things as she replaced the bag connected to my IV tube.

"Where am I?" I groaned, feeling weak.

"You're at Windham General Hospital," she smiled sweetly.

I looked at her with my eyes half-shut, "What happened?"

"You had a heart attack, sweetie," she said, fluffing my pillow.

"What?" I said in disbelief. I tried to sit up, but the nurse encouraged me to stay down and rest. "How?" I asked.

"Ask the doctor," she pointed at the doorway as the doctor walked into the room.

"Good to see you awake, Thomas," the doctor said. He had a thick mustache and flat, full hair. He seemed pretty young for most doctors. Beyond that, it was hard to see him clearly with the dim lighting in my room.

"I don't understand, doctor," I said, "How did I get a heart attack? I'm only seventeen."

"Who told you that?"

I pointed at the door, "The nurse."

"Don't listen to that nonsense. She's no doctor," he replied.

"So," I asked, "what did I get?"

"Well, you have quite a high blood pressure for someone your age. I'm guessing that at least one of your parents has a history of that as well. Often times, something like severe emotional stress, along with plaque buildup in your arteries, can further obstruct blood flow and induce a heart attack. And the ambulance rushed you here in around ten minutes, but you appeared to be much better soon after we put you in this bed," he reported jubilantly.

"What happened, then?" I asked again, growing more frustrated.

"Considering that you're a pretty healthy kid, I can only guess it was an unpredictable heart spasm, totally random. Or, something completely different and unknown." he explained while flipping through charts at the foot of my bed, "I'd like to have some specialists study you over the course of the next few months to determine the source of your symptoms. Is that all right?"

"Is this going to happen again?" I ignored his question.

"The heart issue? That depends. They are, however, unlikely to reoccur, although I'd also like to prescribe you some medicine. Interestingly, I've never heard of your situation before." I didn't believe that this man was qualified, given that he wasn't sure what happened to me, needed specialists to diagnose my issue, and planned on blindly prescribing me meds.

The doctor further went on to tell me how proper eating, physical activity, and stress management therapy with a psychiatrist could help me stay healthy for the remainder of my life. He also asked me some questions that may help with explain the cause, but I told him nothing helpful.

"You have some visitors, too, from your school. Will you be all right to let them come by?"

"Sure," I nodded.

Micky walked in slowly with his hands in his pockets. He looked ashamed and contrite, something that I never imagined I'd witness in my life. "Hey, Tommy boy," he said quietly, keeping his head down.

"Hey, Micky," I said, trying not to think about anything serious. It was just nice to see a familiar face. Just like that, my pain eased up, and it felt like my mind relaxed a little.

"Look, Tommy boy," he said after some silence, "I'm really sorry, about everything."

I attempted to sit up and smile. "It's okay Micky. It wasn't your fault," I laughed, "I can't believe what had just happened, though. Who's ever heard of that?"

"I knew you were a special kid," he joked.

Throughout the day, Micky came in to check on me, as well as one of the deans, who would supervise me during my stay at the hospital. When the nurse told me that Dr. Carter and Fitzgerald wanted to come visit me, I told her that I'd prefer it if they just stayed away.

My mother was driving down to see me, but my father couldn't be reached. It was hard to deal with, but it just seemed all too wild. After a couple of days, I was released—with blood pressure medication—from the hospital and driven back to Kingsley by my mother, who was all too worried for me.

The doctor had signed me up for appointments with a specialist in order to confirm the diagnosis, but as far as I was concerned, I was fine, physically speaking.

People who saw and recognized me gave cautious, respectful glances before gossiping and wondering about my hospitalization behind my back. Elise was waiting in my dorm room when I returned. "Hi, Tommy," she spoke softly, wearing a bright green dress, "Micky let me in. How are you?"

"You don't have to talk to me like a toddler," I replied stoically, "I'm fine."

We talked for a little bit, but she left after a short while. I think that the trip to the hospital was exactly what I needed to calm myself. Everything that had happened, though, was still just hard to comprehend. It wasn't stress that caused it, though. It was pain.

After she had left my room, I sat there, hearing only the pounding of my heart. It was this one moment of quietude and solitary tranquility that I had daydreamed about lustfully on the many stressful nights that took my being away from me. The minutes felt like hours while I tried to soak in every moment, as I knew that the moment I stepped out of my room for the last time, I would enter the long tedium life—adorned with an illusion of success—which many would envy. In truth, all I desired was to live completely alone in some spacious mountain valley or near a peaceful river, yet I knew that I had a personal responsibility to continue my predetermined, morally deprecating journey. Still, I would always feel an incomplete satisfaction. To me, achieving true happiness would be sampling true success, an idea that Kingsley managed to diminish in its students. It is unfortunate that I am trapped in a web of sorrow, eternally bound to suffer from the obstacles placed before me. So for twenty long minutes, I sat and relished in the peace amidst the chaos.

Chapter 14

My mother that night took me to a restaurant for dinner. I decided to order a salad, keep the arteries clean like the incompetent doctor suggested. The atmosphere of the place was quiet and private, with only soft sounds of conversation as back noise. People on dates would discuss the delectability of the meals in order to fill the awkward space, while parents in families would scold their kids for playing with their food.

With a cold, silver fork, I pushed pieces of lettuce around. Neither of us spoke for nearly ten minutes straight, trying to delay the inevitable talk, until finally, my mother made a futile attempt to distract me. "So," she smiled, "Are you glad to be out of the hospital?"

I looked up at her. Seeing that she wouldn't confront the subject but rather cower shamelessly, I spoke up, "Why did you cheat on dad?"

She seemed surprise, as if I was going to avoid the topic the entire night. "Thomas, dear, lower your voice," she instructed. Her entire life, she had always worried about her reputation and what others thought of her instead of seeing what she thought of herself.

"Please, just answer the question," I pleaded, calmly, "I was hoping that my hospitalization would've been enough to get a truthful answer out of you, for once."

Checking around to ensure that no acquaintance or Kingsley parent was near, she set her fork and knife down.

"I'm sorry, Thomas," she said, "I wanted to tell you, I really did." She proceeded to tell my father's story, about how he was never there for my mother or me.

"You're right, about him. But, that still doesn't give you the reason to do something like that," I refuted, "how'd this idea even ever come into your mind, especially with Dr. Fitzgerald?" I felt like my mother had become the child, and I, the parent.

Her face flushed with guilt, "It was when you had first looked at applying for boarding schools. Your father knew George when he attended, and so he invited him over for dinner. He was the nicest, most pleasant man I'd ever met. I would never have done anything, but your father just became more and more distant, and after that dinner, I continued to speak to him. First, it was about you and your admissions, and then it was just, conversation. I hadn't spoken so freely with anyone for years."

It pained me to comprehend it, but I knew the feeling well. Maybe it was the way I was raised, or just the life I was born into, but there had never been anyone for me to talk to, unrestrained, for years.

"Besides," she continued, "From what I've heard, George has been meticulous to make sure you do well at Kingsley, also."

I didn't say anything, but only thought to myself. Did I even earn my way into the Red Clock Order, or did this feeble man get me into the society? If that was true, then everything was all a lie.

I wasn't angry anymore, just saddened. "I think that I should change schools," I told my mother. It didn't require much contemplation to decide that that would be best.

Predictably, she was surprised and denied my request at first, while wondering what would catalyze such an action. So, I excluded the mention of the Red Clock Order but explained in good detail about how it was just a poor environment to study in and apply to college.

She called my father, who, in turn, angrily lectured me on my ridiculous proposal to switch out of Kingsley. "Talk to your son, for once," I heard my mom beg over the phone. Maintaining my calm, I told him about everything, without restraint. "This is everything that you missed after not calling," I told him, deadpan.

He sighed, and I could hear all the tension and disappointment in that one, brief exhale. I felt terrible, but my father eventually, yet reluctantly, agreed. It didn't take much to convince him upon mentioning the Red Clock Order, and my own, undeserved role in it.

While trying to keep my leaving a secret, Fitzgerald entered my room to talk to me in private about my future. However kind or good-hearted this man was, I still had no interest whatsoever to talk to him. So he spoke, and I listened.

"Your mother told me about you leaving," he said softly, "I understand your reasoning. However, you'll always have a place at Kingsley, and you'll always be a part of the Red Clock Order, regardless."

I scoffed. I was never truly a part of the club, the society, the cult. He paused and continued, "The club has connections with many other boarding school administrators and admissions offices. So just fill out the applications over the summer, and I can guarantee you some options for your senior year. It's not too difficult, either, combined with your exceptional academic record."

During his monologue, I sat on my bed, slouched. "I know this has all been hard, Thomas, and for that, I'm sorry.

I hope that, one day, this can all be put behind us," he said as he stood up from the chair, "I'll see you later."

After he left, my eyes swelled up in tears, in regret of my life, and my misfortune. For the rest of the night, I sat on my bed and wept, feeling like a vulnerable child. What a fucking life, I thought to myself.

Chapter 15

The last couple weeks of school went by in a flash. Students soaked in the sun while studying outside with some minor distractions. Although I'd never be returning, I figured it'd be better to go out with a bang.

So I stuck to my original study habits while Micky consistently kept to himself and his work. I don't know if it was my heart problems, or just a parting gift by the universe, but Micky had finally stopped disappearing at odd hours and pestering me at night. The tranquility was blissful and pleasant.

Dr. Carter stuck to his duties as a house counselor and only acknowledged me when it was necessary. Herman was, hopefully, out of my life for good, too. For once, things seemed normal, as the random calamities seemed to have come and gone, leaving me with only a permanent scar of shame, written into my mind.

Final exams ended, but I really couldn't care about my grades, except for a small flickering desire to compete with myself to do better. As I spent the last few days packing my items up into boxes, I tried to take in every scent and image of Kingsley. Even though I hated the school with a burning passion, three of my years had been invested into the godforsaken school, and memories of it would be something that stuck with me forever.

In the late afternoon of a Friday, the day before most students were required to leave, a knock came from my door. The shapely, blond-haired, green eyed figure of Elise walked in slowly.

She asked if I would be attending the graduation ceremony. I wouldn't. "So this is probably the last time I'll see you," she said.

We shared an awkward conversation about the future, and she left with an embrace. I wondered if I would ever see her again. As for Micky, before he departed for the drive home, I left him with a nod, as we both diverged onto separate paths.

"I have to face my fucking parents, who will probably berate me on the consequences of weed. Fuck," he still had a smile on his face, "I'll see you next year, Tommy boy."

Micky was still unaware of my departure from the school. It was depressing, to say the least. Micky was planning on moving to a single in the same dorm, without inquiring about my own plans for boarding, next year. He never told me about the results of his disciplinary committee meeting, and I never asked. The last I ever saw of him was when he left my room with a colloquial salute.

To save space in the car, I threw out half of my items. After all my clothes and supplies had been packed away into rectangular cardboard boxes, I asked Mr. Gerald to check my room for cleanliness. However, he was busy checking another student's room upstairs, and so I was forced to ask Dr. Carter for assistance.

Carter scanned my room, looked through shelves, and didn't find a speck out of place. "You're all set, Mr. Walther," he said, shaking my hand, "Watch out for yourself. You won't have Dr. Fitzgerald watching over you at your school anymore."

"You know I'm leaving?" I asked.

"Fitzgerald asked me to call the other schools about your future next year," he responded. He looked at me intently,

"I hope that you make the best of what's left of your life, Mr. Walther."

Without an extraneous word, he left. Even now, I still have not figured out what his thoughts about me were.

Leaving Elise, leaving Micky, Kingsley, and the Red Clock Order, all felt too simple, too easy. Given all the past incidents, it seemed anticlimactic, as if I should've left with a bigger bang. Alas, my exit wasn't celebrated or mourned; I didn't get back together with Elise or say my last farewell to Micky.

Instead, I packed my boxes into the limousine that my mother called to pick me up, put one foot into the car, and took one last look at the campus. I sat down inside the limousine, with the scent of fresh leather, and left. There was nothing left for me at Kingsley, except a vault of bad memories, which I hoped to seal away forever.

Over the summer, my mother started packing and moving her stuff out of the house to live with Fitzgerald. My father, deciding that since I spent most of my time at school and he could care less about a large yard, hired a real estate agent to sell the old home. Both my parents would receive joint funds for the earnings of the sale. My father also, with his plentiful savings earned from endless work, bought a penthouse in the upper East side of Manhattan to cut his commute short.

As the small items that once defined my home vanished into storage boxes, the house gradually emptied. Eventually, it just looked like any other house, without the many refrigerator magnets, family vacation pictures, or even the unopened letters lying on the kitchen counter.

Early into the break, Fitzgerald registered me for an exclusive ten-student intensive program taught at Columbia. My mother urged me to attend, telling me that the program would be exceptionally beneficial. With nothing else to do for the early summer, I agreed, and spent five weeks in New York. I recognized three of the other students, who were Red Clock recruits and soon-to-be official members. They nodded at me but kept to themselves. One confronted me about dropping out of the society meetings but redacted his question when I refused to respond about it.

The three students stuck together, while the rest of the students were aspiring Republican politicians that spent all of their time reading about re-election plans or new taxing plans in the paper. After the first day, I decided to stay at my father's penthouse instead of the dreary college housing. At night, I spent half of my allotted sleeping time questioning how I got to where I was.

In the five weeks, tutors with doctorates taught us to refine our public speaking, to improve writing skills, and—for the cherry on top—a few introductory lessons on the stock market, something that the politic-philes disapproved of until the teachers explained how learning it would enhance their knowledge in economics. By the time it was all said and done, I still felt the same. It was a waste of five weeks to wake up every morning, take the subway or a cab, and sit in front of a chattering teacher who probably charged a few thousand dollars for the course.

At night, I would work on my applications and essays for a transfer, which I completed in a short time span. Following the instructions, I mailed it to Kingsley and the folder was probably handed to Fitzgerald and the Red Clock. In only a few days, my mother mailed back six different large envelopes with first class mail stamps on them. All of the schools that I had applied to accepted in less than two weeks, which I assumed was not because of my high marks, which were standard on any prep school student's application.

After spending weeks studying and reading over the packets sent by each school, I finally decided on Andover, pleased with its acreage and small town setting, as well as its small class sizes. For the rest of the summer, I spent my days sitting at Nantucket, biking occasionally, but mostly sleeping. Every other week, I would see a specialist, typically a cardiologist, who would examine me, run tests, and ask questions. Eventually, they determined my condition possibly something called broken heart syndrome. Still, though, they were uncertain and instructed me to call them, should anything unusual occur again.

When school had finally begun, the differences from Kingsley were vast. The workload wasn't smaller, yet the teachers were nicer, the students were normal, and waking up wasn't as depressing as I had expected it to be. I don't know what it was, but the skies just didn't seem as hazy as before. Maybe Kingsley was just hidden behind its own abstruse shroud of gloom and despair. Nevertheless, I stepped into the year with a shy but large stride.

In the fall, I applied to Harvard, Princeton, Yale, and other top colleges without many outstanding extracurriculars. My grades were still strong, my athletics were acceptable, and my SAT scores averaged in the high ninetieth percentiles. I mailed out the applications, attended the interviews, and crossed my fingers.

The seasons passed by in a flash, without any sarcastic teacher or weird, financially-based secret societies. As the spring term ended, my neighboring dorm mates all shouted in joy at their admissions letters. I jumped and shouted with them after I received my heavy, large envelope with the Yale seal on it. I was seeing bulldog blue, and it was good.

Finally, my efforts had paid off, and luck had arrived to send me off to college. With my past behind me, I entered

Yale with a fresh face and proud smile, as well as an intent to find a major in economics. Fitzgerald was right, though. Kingsley had become a memory, but it was still a present entity in my thoughts.

Because I rarely spoke to Fitzgerald, who eventually became my stepfather, even during the holidays, I never figured out if the Red Clock Order stuck with me. I did, however, have a gut feeling that the secret society never left, given that I was consecutively accepted into multiple internships and jobs at large investment management firms without rejection. Emotionally, though, the society stayed with me, bringing up mild chest pain every time I thought about it.

My life had become predictable, and yet I still woke up every day, wondering what would come next. With everything that Kingsley had slung at me, I believed that nothing in the future would prove more challenging. Unfortunately, no one had told me about the volatility of the stock market. Nonetheless, I live day-by-day, looking into the future and glancing back at the past.

EPILOGUE

Too often, we overlook the values of life. We ignore the little details of time and experience when, at any second, we could be gone, by God's hand, a criminal's, or even our own. Most are aware of this, yet why do we continue to squander life with pointless activities when so much has been unexplored? Perhaps it's because we're all insane and we just don't know it yet.

Life was good, so it seemed. At least in the eyes of my corporate inferiors, life seemed superb in comparison. The new promotion seemed all but deserved. After a series of warm pats on the back, which disguised the envious faces of both fresh employees and some older ones, I locked the door to my new office and took a seat in my leather chair, which made crinkling noises that made me cringe. Staring down at my new glass desk, I saw my reflection and a sudden emotion of disgust overwhelmed me. I felt as if my legs were going to force myself out of the high building from the translucent window panes behind me. What genius architect decided to place large single sheets of glass behind an office sixty stories high, anyways? Gently resting my forehead, wrinkled from stress, against the palm of my left hand, I sighed.

Days from The Kingsley School still haunt me. From the moment I read the acceptance letter, I began my steady plummet down towards the fiery bowels of bitter reality that society labels as success. If a newborn, unidentified by the marks of the world, were to see me, he would believe that he was looking into a mirror. The only difference would be my fatigued face, marred by a few incidents, stretched through years. Those scars are the only indications of my character, the only markings that define me.

I woke up from a brief sleep that I fell into unawares. Four hours had passed. I was more tired than I knew, apparently. My phone chirped in long intervals as its screen read three missed calls. I had slept until night.

Standing up from the pristine, black leather armchair, I took my navy blue suit jacket hanging from the seat and walked out. Avoiding as many people as possible, I managed to sneak out of the office virtually unseen. Confrontation, after all, is useless without a progressive purpose. After momentarily standing outside and breathing in the scent of a nearby bakery, I walked inside Grand Central to hop onto the train back to my home, or rather the house that I used to live in but bought back using my father's inheritance.

I spent dinner sitting alone on a dark, long table with leftover sirloin. Still awake from an extensive nap, I quietly meandered around the mostly vacant ground floor of the place until I approached the library. Endless rows of books gathered dust and rested on unreachable curved, high, dark cherry shelves. A single heartwood table, along with two chairs, sat comfortably on soft, mildew-green. Scanning over the texts, most of them meaningless, I descended the stairs, each step creaking louder than the last, and walked towards an important section of my "collection." I could never remember where these yearbooks were, but I always managed to randomly find them among the millions of aged pages that adorned the room. I finally decided to take out a yearbook from my first year, my most serene year, at The Kingsley School.

Continuing towards later years, while carefully replacing the previous books in proper order, I eventually arrived at senior year. My inconsistent grinning died out, and it felt as if a mild gloom snuck behind me. I immediately closed the book and headed upstairs, past the white living room, finally into the kitchen.

Hopeful that some alcohol would cure my throbbing headache, I looked towards my amateur wine collection sitting atop the gray granite countertop. I stared blankly at a bottle of 1945 Pétrus, and decided that it'd be better to open a bottle and drink it instead of letting it rot. It's all for show anyways, wine enthusiasts that claim they taste extreme differences simply evince their pretentiousness.

I drew out a black, steel spinning chair, which made a loud screeching noise against the hardwood floor. Without drinking it, I set down my glass of wine on the cold, black marble countertop and took a heavy sigh. I can never find serenity in guiltlessness.

Since I could never do work once my foot stepped out of the office, I found myself mentally in pain, but physically bored with my self-diagnosed mild insomnia. Minutes later, I unconsciously began sifting through the mail with little to no desire to move any limb save for my arms. By the time the hour hand hit the "one" on the generic black and white clock next to the kitchen cabinets, I had finished all but one piece of mail in the pile. A small, faded yellow-white colored letter lay face down on the countertop. On the front, an ornately decorated white sticker sealed the thick, canvas letter with a blue seal that read "Sigil. Kingsley In Scholis MDCCLXXXIV". My instinctive smile and excitement, upon seeing a familiar name, quickly turned into a somber dejection as painful memories came shooting back.

In an attempt to finish reading it as fast as possible, I immediately opened the folded letter:

"Class of '83 Alumni,

> *Ten years ago, you graduated from a school full of unforgettable memories and irreplaceable camaraderie. The blood and sweat that you put in to your work at The Kingsley School has both left a permanent place on the Oak Room table as well as defined who you are today. Now, it's time to see old friends and rekindle your relationship with your alma mater. You are graciously invited to the Ten Year Reunion of the Kingsley School's Class of 1983 on June 6th, 1994. Please check one of the boxes below to RSVP.*
>
> > *Sincerely, The Kingsley School*
> > *Administrator Maston"*

I chuckled with spite after finishing the letter. No matter how much the school tried to sound friendly, warm, or hospitable, you were always reminded of how they didn't give a rat's ass about you, just one person blurred into the crowd that consisted of hundreds of others. It was funny, though, I didn't even graduate from there.

After contemplating for a few moments, something possessed me. I took a pen from a drawer in the counter and neatly marked an "x" in the box next to "I will be attending".

Each of the following weeks proved dryer and more unexciting than the last, with work piled up to my neck. Only the reunion, which instilled in me both peace and anxiety, provided me with the interruption from my disgustingly habitual life. On the morning of June 6th, I headed out on a three-hour drive to Kingsley in Windham, Massachusetts, not exasperatingly longer of a drive than my everyday commute to Manhattan.

Windham was more so a small, dainty village than an actual town. A few large houses could be found in random, peculiar areas of the town. The only truly busy area was the oasis of downtown, filled with shops, a five-minute walk from campus. Kingsley laid in the center of Windham, next to a lake, named Good Plains Lake likely by some sardonic adventurers in the colonial era, close to the mountains. After circling around for a few minutes inan attempt to find the school on the forest-covered roads, I finally reached the hidden driveway that led to campus.

As insouciant laughter suffocated the humid air, a warm zephyr blew by and seemed to quiet down the grass fields. Five minutes into the reunion, it was blatant to most that few felt pure joy to see their old friends again. A white banner that read "Class of '83, Kingsley School" loomed above flimsy tables that rested on a grassy plain. The lawn was filled with small talk and airy music. Various alumni shared short glances with each other, only by accident while nervously looking around. I scanned the serene plains and felt out of place on what was once rolling hills but had been converted into flat sports fields. It was not so much the physical change of the campus that saddened me, but the scars that engraved the campus grounds.

Halfway into the reunions, I managed to tear off my name sticker, sneak past the throngs of people and walk into the main campus. Ivy leaves lazily clung to the ancient, faded grayish-red brick walls of the buildings. Over years, it seemed that the school still cared little for the stability that modern architecture could provide and valued only the exterior beauty that antiquity gave to the buildings. Some students remained on campus to stay and attend commencement and reunions, as a few did at the end of each year. Their innocent, jovial attitudes made me feel a depressed envy towards them.

Almost instinctively, I found my way across the large grassy quad where the campus was centered. Ten years had gone by and the school still didn't bother to cut the grass to proper length. I ended up in front of Galloway House, a small rectangular building with a red and white brick exterior with small windows that could barely let a person through. This two-story building had once hosted a myriad of many midnight meetings and hazings, perhaps too many.

I walked up to the door of Galloway House and turned the doorknob. I was surprised that the building had not been destroyed, let alone left in such good condition. My nervousness prevented me from opening the door. Part of me didn't want to relive the memories, but I knew that I was going to force myself to go inside one way or another. So I took a heavy sigh, opened the door, and entered the first room.

In an instant, the images of intricate chandeliers and oak tables that always had a scent of fresh pine vanished. What replaced those thoughts were flimsy desk chairs that had inappropriate etchings on their surfaces. A single blackboard hung on the left side of the room and dust smothered the dark walls.

I made my way through the forest of tattered green carpet and approached the door leading up to the second floor at the other end of the room. The door was missing a handle and looked like it had been victim to an abusive man whose only true fault was his own passion. Its ornate carvings had been lost underneath its paint chips and damaged face. It's truly a shame that it couldn't live the remainder of its years in solitary tranquility. It looked like the entire house had been abandoned, meaning the society disbanded or simply moved.

While brushing off the dust and dirt from my loafers before heading upstairs, I heard some footsteps on the thin floor above. Hastily, I stumbled over to the left corner of the room, whether by instinct or by some other anomaly I'm still unsure.

A man with a gray blazer and dark pants opened the broken door slowly as it creaked in despair. He walked a few steps forward, put his drink down on a dusty table and leaned against the wall to clean his loafers. Before long, he noticed me, unmoving, standing in the corner of the building. "Can I help you?" he asked without alarm.

"Sorry," I unfroze from my paralyzed position.

The man walked towards me slowly and reached out his fragile arm for a handshake, "No need for apologies. I'm David." His old age and thin voice deceived his personality. His face was all too familiar, yet I was just a little bit short of identifying the man. After a few years of reading the faces of businessmen, I could tell that this man was more well established than he let on at first appearance.

"I'm Thomas, Thomas Walther," I replied, without trying to discover his last name. It wasn't important, anyways.

He paused and his eyes regained some sheen for a moment before he nodded, "Nice to meet you, Mr. Walther."

"Please," I extended in courtesy, "call me Thomas." He stared at the door for a while before speaking again.

"So," his voice, however quiet, surprised me out of the silence, "if I may ask, what are you doing here in Galloway House?"

"Just revisiting old memories, ones that I prefer buried," I laughed, "I'm just kidding." I wasn't kidding. The building just drew me over, possessing me like some universal spirit to laugh at my past.

"Are you here for the reunion?" I asked, although I assumed that he was some faculty member given his age.

"No, no," he laughed, "I am, however, a stepfather of an alumna."

"Really," I nodded, "who is he?"

"She," he corrected, "her name is Elise Poitier."

I laughed in disbelief. The world seemed to have a fondness for putting cruel coincidences on me. The man, only ten years later, looked completely different. What was left of his hair had thinned out. His face looked thirty years older than the last time I saw him, and he appeared much thinner and weaker.

"Would you care to join me outside? This windowless room is far too stale to withstand," Elise's father asked as if my past was nothing of importance.

"Sure," I replied, without a drink in hand.

We both were unbearably silent for a few minutes until a few students passed by. Two of them were in clean pressed suits while the other was in a short dress. He finally started speaking, following another sip from his dry whiskey, "The attire of these young women shrinks more every year, don't they? I remember when ankle-length clothes were popular in the summer when I was young. Admittedly, though, I spent more time flirting with girls than actually conversing when I was in high school. I can't say that I didn't enjoy it, though."

"Well, time's change, but people never do," I reflected.

"I'm sure," he said with a grossly condescending tone.

I failed to control my own words, "Sir, I'm not sure if you remember me, but I was friends with your daughter. I was in the Order, too."

"I know," he replied nonchalantly as he took a sip from his glass of what appeared to be whiskey. With a hand in his pocket and his eyes staring blankly at the door in a sophisticated stance, he looked like the spitting image of my father. "You were the most insolent student I had ever faced."

"How is Elise?" I asked impatiently. This man really didn't like to cut to the chase and face the inevitable, "I haven't seen her since she graduated."

"Since you ruined my daughter's life?" he falsely accused in his calm manner, an attitude that was quickly become annoying.

"Sir," I said to Herman, "Mr. Herman, I have no idea what you're talking about. I didn't ruin your daughter's life."

"Of course you didn't," he said sarcastically, "I never trusted you, to begin with." He took a sip from his glass.

"Just remember," He continued, "Mr. Walther, Fitzgerald may still consider you a Red Clock alumnus, but as far as I'm concerned—or Dr. Carter, or even the rest of the society, for that matter—you are not a part of the Order."

I never really wanted to be a part of the Red Clock Order to begin with.

"David," a woman's voice from afar interrupted my response. Herman and I both looked over at the source of the voice.

Elise, in a seemingly expensive, but not ostentatious, bright dress walked up from across the quad of main campus. She had matured not in an aged but a more refined manner. She looked beautiful and elegant at the same time. I failed to stifle a smile as a feeling of emotions surfaced, ones that had been buried for a while. My sentimentality had improved substantially since Kingsley, apparently.

"David," she approached, "my mother is looking for you. She wants you to meet one of Harlow's old classmate's parents. They are thinking about taking their yacht around the Atlantic as well."

"Thank you, my dear," he glared over at me as he stepped away from the door.

"Who's your friend?" she asked as she pointed over at me. With a quick study of me, her eyes widened in recognition, "Thomas? Tommy Walther?"

"Elise," I greeted her, completely surprised.

We hugged as she kept her drink raised in her left hand. "I haven't seen you in ages. How've you been?"

211

"I've been good," I responded, rather detached, "I'm guessing you're here for Harlow's reunion?". She nodded.

We went through the niceties, asking about each other's lives. She actually declined Princeton and graduated from Brown with a degree in journalism after deferring a year. She was now interning at the New York Times.

I explained to her, in turn, about my life after Kingsley. "Really? You transferred somewhere else for senior year? I had no idea. Where'd you go?" she spoke as if everything was completely casual, but the matter being discussed was, to me, very serious. She asked me about my heart condition, and I told her that I'd never been healthier.

I informed her about Andover my senior year, and how its experience was entirely different from Kingsley. After a couple minutes of conversation, though, Herman's words were still in my head.

"So what were you and David talking about?" she asked, filling the silence.

"I'm not quite sure. He was just mentioning how I ruined your life or something to that effect? I guess he still doesn't like me. But, I have to know, did you defer because of me?"

Her laugh was gentle and formal, "No. You know David. He likes to exaggerate, especially when it has to do with my life. I should've told you that I decided to defer, and I was going to, but you were pretty upset at me, from what I recall. And then, you went to the hospital, and I didn't get a chance to actually talk to you."

I apologized. "I had a pretty short temper, back then."

"Don't be sorry," she said, "I've heard worse. Anyways, David was pretty upset with me. I deferred to spend time in Europe to study art and history, life dreams and all, which he was rather upset with. Then I went to Brown instead of Princeton, and now I'm a journalist intern and not a med student or working at some investment bank like David's ideal. I still couldn't care less, I love what I do." Elise sounded like she had accomplished my aspirations, someone who lived carefree and pursued a passion. I was envious.

"So," she ventured intrepidly into an uneasy subject, "How's Micky? Have you talked to him since he left?"

"Since he graduated from here? No, I haven't."

She paused and stuttered hesitantly, "You know he didn't graduate, right?"

I chuckled nervously, "What do you mean. Did he drop out?"

She grew tense and sighed, "Well, when I went to Harlow's graduation, I tried to look for you. When I couldn't find your name on the list of the graduating class members, I looked for Micky, hoping to ask him about you."

"So, he just left?" I interrupted.

She chuckled in the interim of uncomfortable silence, "Well, when I saw Dr. Carter, I thought to ask about you two. He didn't seem to want to talk about you, but he told me that you decided to leave on your own accord. Then he told me about Micky."

"And?"

"The DC committee decided that he leave the school for his marijuana use, Tommy," she told me, "he went back to Washington and went to a local school near Potomac . . . Maryland."

I sighed and didn't know what to say. After a few minutes of taciturnity, she asked me about my job, and slowly, we drifted away from the subject of Micky.

After a short while, we returned to the crowds on the lawn, and the party had seemed to gradually come to an end. "Listen," she said, taking a permanent marker and writing her number down on a blank nametag sticker, "I'm pretty busy on the weekdays, but give me a call some time for lunch, maybe. We can thoroughly catch up then."

I took the sticker and looked up at her grinning face. Instinctively, I took the paper. "I'll be sure to call," I smiled back.

So there it ended, a glimmer peeking out from the burnt ashes of my time at boarding school. I couldn't help but wonder if others had it as difficult, but it was unlikely. The stress was not difficult to hide, save for the physical manifestations such as the grayed hair and wrinkles, but no man could ever conceal the challenges of the greed and jealousy that the Order provoked. I was incapable, unwilling to face myself, and so I failed. Nevertheless, no obstacle I confronted was ever as difficult as the workload from Kingsley. While I never fully valued the honor of taking my first steps onto the Kingsley lawn, a sharp coat of nostalgia accompanied me as I took my last. When people say that your time at boarding school is for life, for better or for worse, they're right.

About the Author

Kevin Ma is currently a student of the class of 2013 at Phillips Academy Andover, a reputable preparatory boarding school in Andover, Massachusetts. He is a dedicated student with high marks and a number of leadership positions in his extracurricular activities, including UNICEF club and Business and Finance Forum.

When away from school, he lives at home in Greenwich, Connecticut with his mother and stepfather and greatly enjoys spending his summers at his family's summerhouse on Martha's Vineyard.

Kevin also has an older sister, a Deerfield Academy and Princeton University alumnus who is currently a medical student at NYU.

Outside of school, Kevin prefers to pursue his interests through a variety of internships and programs. He most aspires to obtain a future in the field of finance, a subject for which he possesses an outstanding passion. Most recently, he worked a as an intern for five weeks at a private equity firm in Beijing, China where his dad lives.